BLACK OPS.

JUNGLE KILL

JIM ELDRIDGE

EGMONT

*For Lynne, without whom this would
never have been written.*

EGMONT

We bring stories to life

Black Ops: Jungle Kill
First published 2010
by Egmont UK Limited
239 Kensington High Street
London W8 6SA

Text copyright © 2010 Jim Eldridge

The moral rights of the author have been asserted

ISBN 978 1 4052 4780 1

1 3 5 7 9 10 8 6 4 2

www.egmont.co.uk

A CIP catalogue record for this title is available
from the British Library

Typeset by Avon DataSet Ltd, Bidford on Avon, Warwickshire
Printed and bound in Great Britain by the CPI Group

1

The pistol in Paul Mitchell's hand was an H&K Mark 23. The man Mitchell was pointing it at stood with his hands clasped to the top of his head, sweat and blood running down his face. He looked terrified.

'This is the Mark 23,' Mitch told the man coolly, 'one of the finest guns in the world. Right now it's fully loaded and fixed with a silencer. No one will hear it if it fires.'

The man glanced around agitatedly. He had come at Mitch out of the bushes surrounding the building just a few minutes before, levelling an assault rifle. A Kalashnikov – the AK-47. He should have shot Mitch then, and his troubles would have been over. But he'd thought Mitch was unarmed.

That was his first mistake. His second mistake was to assume that because Mitch looked young he would have no real fighting experience. Mitch *was* young, but he'd served in the army since he was seventeen. And his last year had been with Special Forces.

The man's third mistake was to step towards Mitch and poke him in the chest with the end of the rifle barrel. Never do that to someone who's been Special Forces trained. First rule of pointing a gun at anyone: if they appear unarmed, there's no need to put yourself within reach of them. Mitch had knocked the Kalashnikov to one side then kicked the man in the groin. As he went down Mitch snatched the rifle from him and hit him in the face with the butt.

Mitch had then dumped the Kalashnikov on the ground and pulled out the Mark 23. 'I'm going to throw a mobile phone on to the ground near you,' Mitch said calmly, keeping the pistol aimed firmly at the man's head. 'You're going to bend down and pick it up. This gun will be aimed at your head the whole time. If you attempt to make a run for it, or use the mobile phone as a weapon or a diversion, I will shoot you. Is that clear? Nod if you understand.'

The man nodded slowly. Mitch reached into his pocket, took out a mobile phone and gently tossed it so it landed on the gravel.

'You can take your hands off the top of your head, but spread them. Keep them away from your body. Bend down and pick up the phone.'

The man hesitated, then did as he had been told. Mitch kept the gun on him, not wavering.

'Dial Mr Zakhovsky's private number.'

'I don't have it,' the man began, but he shut up abruptly when he saw the expression on Mitch's face.

'Believe me, mate,' Mitch snapped, 'if you don't have it then you're no use to me and I might as well kill you right now. So, let's try that again. Dial Mr Zakhovsky's private number.'

The man began to dial, his hands shaking as he did so. He was obviously scared of what Mr Zakhovsky would do to him. But Mitch was the one holding a gun on him right now.

He finished dialling and held the phone out to Mitch, but Mitch shook his head and gestured for him to put it to his own ear. When the person on the other end of the line answered, he began to stammer out an apology in Russian.

'Stop,' Mitch ordered. 'Tell him Paul Mitchell is here.'

The man said something more in rapid Russian, then listened, nodding. He held out the mobile to Mitch.

'Mr Zakhovsky wants to talk to you.'

'OK,' said Mitch. 'Put the phone on the ground, put your hands back on your head and then step back six paces. Slowly.'

The man complied with the order. Mitch followed, equally slowly, keeping the gun trained on the man's face. When Mitch reached the phone he bent down, picked it up and put it to his ear, still aiming the gun.

'Hello! Hello!' a voice was saying impatiently.

'Mr Zakhovsky,' said Mitch. 'I understand you want to see me.'

'How did you get into my private residence?' the man on the other end of the phone demanded angrily.

'That's my business,' answered Mitch. 'I'll be waiting for you tomorrow at ten a.m. in the lobby of the Excelsior Hotel in Knightsbridge. I think you know it.'

Mitch was taking no chances. Zakhovsky owned quite a few hotels in London but the Excelsior Hotel wasn't one of them. There'd be little chance of him rigging an ambush there at such short notice. Zakhovsky would come with his own protection, of course, but Mitch would be prepared.

There was a pause, then, 'Very well,' Zakhovsky snapped tersely, 'I will see you tomorrow at ten a.m.'

5

'Good,' said Mitch.

'And one more thing,' Zakhovsky sneered. 'The fool you are holding at gunpoint. He has failed me. Kill him.'

'Oh no, Mr Zakhovsky,' replied Mitch, smiling. 'I don't work for you yet. We'll talk about it tomorrow.'

As Mitch hung up, he bent down and picked up the Kalashnikov.

'You can go now,' he told the man. 'Keep walking away from me for a count of one hundred. Slowly. Keep your hands on your head. Don't look back. If you do, I'll have to shoot you. Understood?'

The man nodded. He looked like he was going to collapse with relief.

'Go,' said Mitch.

The man turned and began walking away, hands still on his head. Mitch gave him a count of ten and then made his exit, back the way he'd come.

2

It had all begun when Zakhovsky's private secretary had contacted Mitch a few days earlier and asked him to visit Zakhovsky at his mansion in Regents Park. He had told Mitch that Mr Zakhovsky had some bodyguarding work he'd like to talk to him about.

Mitch had agreed to meet Zakhovsky, and had then hit the Internet to find out more about his potential client. He already knew a little because the press liked to document Zakhovsky's wheelings and dealings, but he knew he'd get more after digging on the web.

Cutting through a lot of rubbish, Mitch had learnt that Leonid Zakhovsky was a Russian who'd made millions – no, make that *billions* – as the major shareholder of a large energy firm in Russia. When the Russian government began demanding large sums of money from him in taxes, Mr Zakhovsky had moved to Britain, taking most of his money with him.

But none of that explained why. Zakhovsky wanted to see Mitch. Zakhovsky lived in a huge mansion in the heart of London, protected by state-of-the-art security equipment and with a bunch of Russian heavies at his disposal. But business was business, and a billionaire with money to throw around was always an attractive proposition, so Mitch decided not to question it further.

Then just as Mitch had been getting ready to call on Zakhovsky he'd received a text message. The message had been brief: 'Danger at Zakhovsky house.' Even stranger, the text had been in Igbo, one of the tribal languages of Nigeria. Why? Who knew Mitch well enough to know that he spoke Igbo?

Mitch had gone to Zakhovsky's house anyway, but undercover, his curiosity aroused. And so far his curiosity had paid off. But that was yesterday.

At the Excelsior, Mitch waited as arranged. It was one of those old-fashioned-looking hotels: wood panels, tubs of flowers, cushioned armchairs and settees in the lobby. But behind the scenes the Excelsior was one of the most hi-tech hotels in London, especially when it came to its security and surveillance system – which was one of the reasons Mitch had chosen it for his meeting with Zakhovsky. Still, he made sure that he kept to the basic rules for his own protection, drilled into him during his time in the SAS.

Rule Number One: never sit with your back to the door.

Rule Number Two: never sit near a window, especially a large one. The view may be great but if a bomb goes off outside the flying glass will kill you if the force of the explosion doesn't.

Rule Number Three: choose a place where you can see the whole room without having to swivel your head from side to side. If you can, pick a corner where two solid walls meet. Brick and concrete. Bullets will tear through stud walls and plasterboard as if they are made of paper.

Mitch chose an armchair in a corner of the room, not low and comfortable, but high-seated enough that he could dive out of it if necessary.

A waitress came over to him, so he ordered a still mineral water, with ice and lemon. He had no intention of drinking it. For all he knew, Zakhovsky had someone in the kitchen on his payroll, ready to slip a little something into anything he ordered, but he knew you can't sit in the lobby of a place like the Excelsior with no drink in front of you without drawing attention to yourself. The perfect cover was to blend into the surroundings. Be invisible.

Mitch checked his watch. One minute before ten. No sign of Zakhovsky. Mitch wondered if the billionaire would come on his own. He doubted it. Very rich people rarely went anywhere on their own. They always had to have a few bodyguards. Plus a lawyer or two. And someone to carry their money.

The waitress returned with his mineral water and the bill. She gave Mitch a smile, putting them on the small table beside him.

Mitch returned her smile then watched her walk away, all the time wondering if someone was going to use her arrival by his chair as a distraction. But no one seemed to be doing anything unusual. No hands went into inside pockets, no one ducked behind one of the ornate columns. Everything seemed normal and safe. But Mitch knew that there was no such thing in his line of work.

Whether Zakhovsky would actually show up at the Excelsior today depended on how much he needed Mitch. He would be annoyed at having to go through this ritual and Mitch knew that very rich men can be very dangerous when they are annoyed.

On full alert now, his eyes continued to watch the crowds of people passing through the lobby, waiting for the action to happen. It came in the form of a tall black man wearing an overcoat, heading towards Mitch. Everything about the man said 'Special

Forces'. Mitch slid his right hand inside his jacket. The man saw the move and stopped, opening his coat so that Mitch could see he wasn't armed. Mitch gave the slightest of nods, and the man continued walking. He settled down in an easy chair opposite.

'Paul Mitchell,' said the man with a smile. 'Good to meet you.' He was American. Mid-twenties at the most. East coast accent. Boston, possibly. 'I'm Charles Nelson.'

'Are you a messenger from Mr Zakhovsky?' Mitch asked.

Nelson shook his head. 'No,' he said. 'Mr Zakhovsky won't be joining us.'

Mitch stood up. 'Then I guess our business here is done.'

Nelson held up a hand. 'Whoa there, Mitchell. The fact is Mr Zakhovsky was never coming. He just helped us out by agreeing to act as an intermediary. To set up this meeting.'

'And who exactly are you?'

'Colonel Nelson. US–UK Combined Special

Forces. You might have heard of us.'

USUKCSF. Delta Force and the SAS. Black Ops, thought Mitch. He had heard about them during his time in the SAS, but he'd never actually met any of them. At least, not that he was aware of. And for Nelson to be a colonel at such a young age meant he must be something special.

'I'm out of Special Forces, Colonel,' said Mitch. 'I left four months ago. Check my record.'

'I already have,' said Nelson.

'If you've read it properly, I think you'll see the regiment won't want me back. I killed the wrong guy,' Mitch said. 'At least, as far as they're concerned. To them, I'm trouble.'

'I wouldn't be so sure,' said Nelson. 'Besides, I think there's more to it than that. Want to tell me about what happened?'

'No,' said Mitch. 'But I'm curious why we're having this meeting.'

'You were in West Africa.'

Mitch nodded, then he smiled. 'That text message

in Igbo. It was you.'

Nelson gave a half-smile. 'Not me, someone else who talks Igbo. We wanted to see if you still remembered the language. We have a situation in West Africa.'

Mitch shook his head. 'No, you've got a situation in Nigeria. Igbo is one of the country's languages.'

Nelson smiled. 'I knew you were the right man for this.'

'I'm not the right man,' said Mitch. 'I left the regiment, remember.'

'But this isn't about rejoining the regiment,' persisted Nelson. 'And, even if it was, you wouldn't have a problem. They've looked into what happened. They know the truth. Captain Danvers was –'

Mitch held up a hand to stop him.

'Let's not talk about it,' he said. 'Just get to the point.'

Nelson nodded. 'How are your other Nigerian tribal languages? Yoruba? Hausa?'

'Yoruba, not too bad. Depends where it is.

The dialect's different from region to region.'

Nelson nodded again. If he was impressed, he didn't show it. 'Do you know much about the current situation in Nigeria?' he asked.

Mitch shrugged. 'Civil war, same as always. Rival factions. Mayhem and murder. Oil.'

'Ever heard of a man called Joseph Mwanga?'

Mitch nodded. 'When I was there Mwanga was trying to get some sort of unified government together. Yoruba, Igbo, Hausa, everyone, all working together.'

'But first he has to get elected,' said Nelson. 'And there are plenty of people who don't want to see that happen.' He paused. 'In our book, Joseph Mwanga is one of the good guys. Problem is he was kidnapped last week.'

'Government, rebels or criminals?' Mitch asked.

'No one's sure,' said Nelson.

Mitch sighed. 'It doesn't matter,' he said. 'He's dead by now.'

Nelson shook his head. 'Not necessarily. There was

a sighting two days ago. One of our spy satellites picked out a group of people moving across an area of bush on foot. Our techies have enhanced it and we're fairly sure that one of the men in the picture is Mwanga. His hands are tied behind his back, but he's on foot, so that means he can walk.'

'How big is the group with him?'

'About twenty. All heavily armed.'

Mitch considered the situation. If Mwanga was still alive, then he was being kept for trade. Either for political reasons, or for money.

'You're going to try to spring him?' asked Mitch.

'Provided we can find him,' replied Nelson, nodding.

'And you want me as part of the team?'

Nelson nodded. 'Standard USUKCSF: three Brits, three Americans,' he said.

Mitch paused. 'Why me?' he asked.

'Because you're Special-Forces trained. You know Nigeria, the country, the languages and the people. You're young and fit, resilient, and you're a survivor. You showed that last night at Zakhovsky's. You could have continued into the house, but you didn't. I liked that thing you did with the mobile phone too. And the fact you never once showed up on the CCTV.'

'How do you know?'

Nelson grinned. 'I was inside the house with Zakhovsky, waiting for you. The plan was for us to talk there.'

'How did you get Zakhovsky to take part in the whole business?' asked Mitch.

'He owes us one,' said Nelson. 'So tell me, Mitch – are you in?'

Mitch thought it over. He'd seen Mwanga just once, when he'd been on leave during a tour of duty in Nigeria. The politician had been making a speech in Kano, the country's second largest city, in which he urged the people to believe in the idea of a government that distributed the country's wealth fairly. Taking from the rich and giving to the poor. An African Robin Hood, in a suit and tie. Mitch had no time for most politicians, but as he'd listened to Mwanga he felt that the man was sincere. He was certainly brave, to talk publicly about taking money away from the wealthy. No wonder someone had kidnapped him. And now Mwanga was a prisoner, and prisoners in West Africa often had very short lives.

There was another reason for signing up. If he was honest, Mitch missed the action. Since leaving the force he'd kept active, mostly bodyguarding, but it hadn't given him that same buzz. He missed being part of a Band of Brothers, guys who loved being in the thick of it, depending on their nerves, adrenalin, and fighting skills to keep them alive. He'd been out of that for too long. Nelson was offering him a way back.

'OK,' he said. 'I'm in.'

3

After that, things moved fast. Mitch and Nelson headed for a secure building within a Ministry of Defence compound in Whitehall. Mitch followed Nelson down to the basement, which looked like a standard briefing room, except for the array of weapons on a large table, which a group of men was examining. The men turned as they came in.

'Guys,' announced Nelson, 'meet Trooper Paul Mitchell, our new unit member. Henceforth to be known as Mitch, unless he's got any objections?'

Nelson looked at Mitch, who shook his head. "Mitch" was fine by him. It was what he'd always been called.

'Mitch, meet Delta Unit. Your own countrymen first: Captain Bob Tait – known as Tug – my second in command.'

Tug was young, five foot seven, serious-looking, with longish fair hair. He nodded and said, 'Welcome,' but there was no accompanying smile. Even in that one clipped word, there was a hint of the upper class that nettled Mitch.

Mitch knew he had a chip on his shoulder about people like Tug. Mitch came from a very poor background on one of London's sprawling, lawless sink estates. People like Tug would never know the daily struggles that people like Mitch had suffered.

'And this is Trooper Danny Graham,' continued Nelson. 'Or Gaz, as everyone calls him.'

Gaz looked about the same age as Mitch and was built like a rugby player, with the broken nose to go with it. He was slightly shorter than Tug, about five six, but much friendlier. He shook Mitch's hand with a firm grip, grinned and said, 'Good to have you aboard, pal!' in a strong accent. Newcastle, Mitch guessed. His hair was cropped so short it was almost just stubble on his bony head. With his build and his shaven skull, Gaz looked like a human version of a pit bull terrier.

At five foot eleven, Mitch knew he himself was tall by SAS standards, almost as tall as the six-foot Nelson.

'Now your American cousins . . .' said Nelson. 'Sergeant Tony Two Moons.'

The taller of the remaining two soldiers stepped forward, his hand held out.

'Welcome to the tribe.' He grinned, shaking Mitch's hand.

'Two Moons.' Mitch nodded. 'Native American?'

'From the Sioux tribe, before the white man persuaded me to join up.'

The others had obviously heard the joke before, but they all grinned, especially the black Colonel Nelson.

'And this is Lieutenant Bernardo Jaurez. Better known as Benny. He's from Texas.'

Benny merely nodded and said: 'Welcome to the unit, Mitch.' No smiles. He was short, thin and wiry

21

and Mitch guessed he was a man who took himself seriously.

Like Tug, Benny looked to be a few years older than Mitch. Early to mid-twenties.

That's two friendly faces, thought Mitch: Two Moons and Gaz. The other two, Tug and Benny, are definitely suspicious of me. The two officers. He wondered if their attitude was because of what had happened with Captain Danvers – all written up in his case file. Mitch didn't blame them – they didn't know the *whole* story. Still, he didn't like talking about it, so he wasn't going to start explaining himself. If they wanted to know what had happened, they could ask.

It was an interesting group: a Sioux Indian, a Hispanic Texan, a Geordie and himself, a Londoner. Where was Tug from? There was definitely something aristocratic about him. Maybe the second son of some titled family. He'd find out later, if it mattered. And the unit was led by the tall, charismatic black colonel from Boston, Massachusetts. Mitch was intrigued.

'OK, introductions over, guys,' said Nelson. 'Five more minutes checking out the hardware, then take your seats for the briefing.' And with that, he headed for the door.

'Where's he going?' Mitch asked.

'Gone to take a leak, I expect,' grinned Two Moons. 'Why?'

Mitch shrugged. 'Just worried he's going to suddenly appear with a bunch of heavies as some sort of test for me.'

Two Moons chuckled. 'You are one suspicious fella, Mitch! You're the one who killed his captain, right?' The rest of the men in the group had moved away.

Mitch hesitated, then shrugged. He'd already guessed that everyone knew what he'd done. Maybe it was best that way.

'Yeah, that's right,' he said.

'On purpose?'

'Right again.'

Two Moons nodded. 'I know how that feels. I killed my sergeant when I was in the regular army, back in the States.'

Mitch was surprised, both at the information, and at how willing Two Moons was to reveal it.

'On purpose?' he asked, echoing Two Moons' question to him.

'Yes and no,' said Two Moons. 'The court martial said it was an accident. But I gotta tell you, Mitch, when I hit that nasty piece of work I may not have been intending to kill him, but I sure as hell wasn't pulling no punches.'

'You killed him with a punch?'

Two Moons nodded. 'One punch,' he affirmed. 'Turns out he had a thin skull. He was also the most racist man I ever met in my whole life. Enjoyed making life miserable for anyone who wasn't pure-bred white. Indians, blacks, Asians, Mexicans – you name it, he hated them. He should never have been made a sergeant in the first place.'

'What happened?' asked Mitch, curious as to

what could have made the friendly Two Moons go so far.

'As I said, he had been making the lives of all of us non-whites a misery,' said Two Moons. 'But I learnt to handle it. Kept my head down and just got on with things. But there was this young black guy from Chicago: skinny kid, seventeen. Brand new. No confidence in himself. Everything he did, this sergeant found fault with and kept punishing him. And I mean *really* punishing him physically. Finally the boy couldn't take it no more and he took a gun and shot himself.

'Well, when I heard that news something inside me sort of snapped, but I still kept my cool. Then, at parade the next morning, this sergeant comes out to give us the official announcement about the kid killing himself, and he makes some sick joke. It so happens that when he said it he was standing right in front of me. If he'd been a few yards either way to my left or my right, I'd have left it. But he was right in front of me, with that stupid grin on his face, and before I knew it: wham! Smack!' Two Moons held up his right fist, and Mitch saw that it looked pretty powerful. 'Got him right between the eyes. End of story. Lucky for me my court-martial decided there'd been strong provocation.' Two Moons gave a wry smile. He paused. 'So that's my story, let's hear yours.'

Mitch shrugged. But before he could say a word they heard Nelson's voice rap out: 'OK, take your seats, guys.'

'I'll tell you about it later,' said Mitch, relieved at the reprieve.

Along with the others, they took their seats in front of a screen fixed to one wall. It showed a map of the Niger Delta. Nelson waited until they were seated, then he addressed them.

'This is Plan A to rescue Joseph Mwanga,' he said. 'And just to let you know, there is no Plan B.' Nelson pointed to a spot east of the Delta. 'This is where Mwanga was last seen, out in the bush, before he and whoever's holding him disappeared into the jungle. Our job is to get in, find him and get him out. One thing's for sure, people will know about us. So, we've fixed up a cover story.

'Spencer-Tado Oil and Gas, one of the many American-British oil companies drilling for oil in the Niger Delta, has recently received threats that some of its employees are going be taken hostage and held to ransom.'

Mitch nodded to himself. Kidnapping for ransom was something that happened all the time in Nigeria. The American or British hostages were generally released when a substantial ransom had been paid, but in a few cases they had been killed and their bodies found floating in the waters of the Delta.

Nelson continued outlining the cover story. 'In view of this it makes sense for Spencer-Tado to hire a bunch of mercenaries as bodyguards to protect their employees. We are that bunch of mercenaries. According to the story that's been spread all over the Niger Delta, we're going to be helicoptered in to guard the onshore oil refinery where the threats were received. As soon as we get there, we're going to go undercover and watch out for the criminals or rebels who've made the threat.

'In fact, the helicopter is going to touch down briefly in the jungle in the eastern area of the Delta, about twenty miles from where Mwanga was last seen, just long enough for us to drop into the jungle. Then the chopper is going to continue its journey to the refinery.

Meanwhile, the hope is that everyone will assume we've been dropped off at the oil refinery and are in hiding, waiting, protecting the oil workers. What we will actually be doing is trekking through the jungle looking for Mwanga and his captors,' concluded Nelson. 'Any questions so far?'

There was a shaking of heads.

'Mitch has been added to the unit because he's served tours of duty in Nigeria, including the Niger Delta. He knows the terrain and he knows the local languages. So he's our ace in the hole.'

Two Moons and Gaz both grinned at Mitch, and

gave him the thumbs-up. Tug and Benny showed no emotion. They definitely don't trust me, thought Mitch.

'OK,' said Nelson. 'That's it. We'll do the rest of the briefing on the plane on the way to Africa. Pack your kit and let's move.'

4

In the minibus on the way to the airfield, Mitch found himself sitting next to Benny Jaurez. They sat in silence as the minibus struggled to make its way through the busy London streets. Mitch looked out of the window, wondering when he'd be back again. Or *if* he would be back.

'Hey, Mitch,' said Benny, the wiry officer. Mitch turned and looked at him. 'Am I right in guessing you got some sort of problem with me?'

'What do you mean?' demanded Mitch, puzzled.

'When the colonel introduced you to us I could see you didn't like me,' Benny continued, his mouth a grim line.

'That's not true,' responded Mitch, annoyed.

'There was definitely something,' insisted Benny.

'I thought at first maybe you were just anti-American, or anti-Latino. Some sort of racist.'

Mitch couldn't help but laugh at this. Him? A racist?

'Yeah, OK.' Benny nodded. 'Then I figured if that was the case you wouldn't want to serve under the colonel. And I saw you talking all friendly with Two Moons so then I think about it, and you were the same with Tug as you were with me. Cold. Distant.' Benny was snapping the straps on his rucksack aggressively now.

Mitch shook his head. 'That's not true,' he said again. 'It was the other way round.'

Benny shrugged. 'Maybe,' he said. 'But I think you've got a thing about officers. You don't like them. That's why you were kicked out of the SAS.'

'I wasn't kicked out, I left,' said Mitch.

'Whatever.' Benny shrugged again. 'The thing is, we're a small and tight unit. Just the six of us. We depend on each other. Every time we go out, our lives are on the line. We protect each other's

31

backs. I don't want to feel you ain't protecting mine because I'm an officer.'

Mitch felt a stirring of anger inside him.

'Listen, *sir*,' he muttered. 'I don't care what rank a man holds. What matters is: do I trust him with my life? In my book, that trust doesn't come automatically because someone's got stripes on their sleeve or brass on their shoulder. That trust comes when I know the man. Comprende, *sir*?'

Benny gave Mitch a hard look. 'Then we'll just have to see how it goes,' he said. 'But let me tell you, Mitch, right now I don't trust you as far as I can spit.'

Mitch nodded. 'Then it's good to know where we stand,' he said. 'That's a start.'

It was another two hours before the men were on board a military plane to Lagos. Mitch took a seat between Two Moons and Gaz near the back of the plane. Nelson, Tug and Benny were near the front.

'First class for officers,' murmured Mitch.

'No, pal,' grinned Gaz. 'Nothing like that. I've fought alongside all these guys.'

'So why are we at the back of the plane?'

'Choice,' said Gaz. 'I always sit at the back of a plane. I've never yet heard of one of these things reversing into a mountain.'

Mitch and Two Moons laughed. But Mitch still felt disappointed there was a gulf between him and Tug and Benny. But he'd just have to live with that. And it was natural that Nelson would sit with his senior officers, planning as they travelled, working out tactics.

'So,' said Two Moons, interrupting his thoughts. 'You said you'd tell me what happened with your captain.'

'OK.' Mitch shrugged. He inhaled deeply. 'It was in Iraq. I was part of a four-man unit, undercover in a place called Mandali, on the Iran–Iraq border.'

'Been there,' Gaz said. 'East of Baghdad.'

Mitch nodded. 'We knew arms and soldiers were coming over the border from Iran. Our job was to find out how, and who was helping them, and target them. What we didn't know, and no one back at HQ had picked up, was that our unit commander, Captain Danvers, was absolutely insane. None of the three of us, me, Johnny and Angel, had worked with him before. None of us even knew anything about him. He was just assigned to us.

'Trouble kicked in almost as soon as we were inserted. Danvers was gung-ho about getting the intel swiftly. So, instead of doing the "hearts and minds" bit with the local tribespeople, he decided to take prisoners and use some muscle on them. Trouble was he had this idea that the people would talk if he threatened their kids.'

Gaz whistled. 'A whole load of trouble,' he said.

'You got it,' agreed Mitch. 'Problem was Danvers didn't just threaten. He took us into this tribal area and told the head man that if they didn't tell us what he wanted to know he'd kill his children. And, to show he meant what he said, he took his gun, aimed it at the head of this fourteen-year-old boy, a nephew of the head man, and pulled the trigger. Bang! One dead kid.'

'He was cracked,' said Two Moons.

'Yup, mad in the head,' agreed Mitch. 'Once he'd done that, there was only one thing to do if we were going to get out of there alive. I put my gun to Danvers' head and shot him there and then. Eye for an eye. That's the way the tribes there see it. As soon as Danvers had pulled the trigger on that kid, any hope of us getting any intel had gone, then or ever after.'

'I can see why you did what you did,' said Two Moons. 'Killing Danvers in front of them was the only way to save the situation.'

'And get out of there alive,' agreed Gaz. 'I've been with those tribes. I know what they're like.'

Mitch gestured towards the front of the plane, where Nelson, Tug and Benny were engaged in whispered conversation. 'Trouble is, the brass don't see it that way. I shot an officer. Makes me dangerous.'

Two Moons shook his head. 'Not here, Mitch,' he said. 'You had no other choice. No one holds it against you in this outfit.'

Mitch shrugged. 'Maybe, maybe not,' he said.

Two Moons leant across Mitch and nudged Gaz. 'So, mate,' he said. 'That's me and Mitch here both with a murky secret. You got any you want to share?'

'Oh, I've got plenty of secrets, mate,' said Gaz, grinning, 'but none that I want to tell the likes of you!'

Mitch and Two Moons laughed. Mitch realised that was the first time in a long while he'd been able to laugh properly. Since he'd shot Captain Danvers, in fact. With a bit of luck, being with these guys could be fun, as well as hard work.

Mitch looked out the window as the plane droned.

'The colonel says you know Nigeria,' said Two Moons after a pause.

Mitch smiled. 'No one knows Nigeria,' he said, chuckling. 'People who say they do are lying. I've done two tours of duty there and it's still a mystery to me.'

'Who runs the country?' asked Two Moons.

'That's the big question,' said Mitch. 'It depends who's in power, and that can change. Basically the place is about civil war, with uneasy political truces now and then to keep some sort of government, and lots of corruption. And, out in the bush, no one runs it.'

'Big corruption?' asked Gaz, interested.

Mitch nodded. 'When one ruler died in suspicious circumstances they found he had several hundred million dollars stashed in different bank accounts.'

Gaz whistled appreciatively. 'Several hundred million,' he said. 'I wouldn't mind laying my hands on a slice of that!'

The plane flew on, hitting a bit of turbulence as it crossed the Atlas Mountains of North Africa, and then settling down for the rest of the journey to Lagos.

Things continued to move fast when they arrived at the Nigerian city. Within fifteen minutes of landing they were strapped into their seats in the bay of a Bell UH-1 helicopter and heading east. Inside the helicopter there was no chance for chatting. The sound of the giant rotors above them made sure of that.

Mitch looked out through the open bay doors of the chopper as it flew over the Delta. As he watched the dense jungle unfold beneath him, he thought about their mission. It wasn't just a case of finding Mwanga. Their biggest problem would be recognising the good guys from the bad guys when they came across them.

When the chopper neared their final landing site Mitch could feel every nerve in his body alert. They were going into trouble. The one question was: how soon would they find it? On a training mission there were always ground rules. You generally knew that, unless you made a stupid mistake, you would come out of it alive. On a real mission the threat of dying was ever-present.

The jungle through the open hatch of the chopper looked like it was getting thicker. Rainforest made for tough terrain. Beneath the thick canopy of green leaves, trees sprang up like weeds from the wet and dark forest floor, the ground uneven and filled with roots twisting like contorted snakes, bursting up out of the soil. One moment you could be on solid ground, the next up to your waist in swamp, with leeches crawling all over you, getting inside your clothes, biting into your skin and sucking your blood.

Then there were the mosquitoes, also looking for blood, and giving you malaria in exchange. Mitch knew disease was the biggest killer in the jungle.

It was a dangerous place, but western companies still came here for one simple reason: oil. Some two million barrels a day were extracted in the Niger Delta. For that kind of money, oil companies were willing to take a risk. Or, at least, they were willing to allow their employees to take a risk. They did as much as they could for their workers. They paid for protection, they spent money locally, they bribed. But not everyone was happy. Some locals were angry that the profits from the oil were going out of the country, instead of helping to solve local problems. Some were furious about the environmental destruction to the Delta.

These were the problems that Mwanga felt he could solve. Colonel Nelson and his superiors obviously believed that Mwanga could solve them too, or they wouldn't be here.

The noise of the rotors whirling overhead filled the chopper bay. Mitch looked around at his comrades. Like him they were kitted out in combat gear with all the gizmos: night-vision goggles, hi-tech headset communication, laser sights on their rifles. And then, of course, their major weapon, the SA80 assault rifle each man held cradled in his arms, ready for use as soon as they hit the ground. The SA80 was perfect as a close-combat weapon: light to carry but powerful and very effective.

In addition, Two Moons was the unit's ordnance and explosives expert and had a range of more powerful weapons and explosives in his kit, including a rocket-propelled grenade launcher and mortars.

Mitch suddenly felt the helicopter bank sharply, and then turn. They were going down. Nelson's voice came through his headphones.

'Here we go, guys!'

The helicopter touched down in a small clearing in the jungle. It took just seconds for the six men to jump down from the open bay doors and head for the trees, where they took cover. The helicopter soared back up into the sky, and roared away, the beat of its rotors drumming against the air. Then it was gone, back towards the refineries and the oil pipelines of the Niger Delta. It was still in view when the firing opened up: bullets from machine guns and rifles pouring into their position. They were under attack.

5

It was the trees that saved them.

The six men threw themselves to the ground, taking what cover they could behind tree roots and gulleys in the uneven jungle floor. The trees around them took most of the damage, wood splinters and chunks of bark flying off as bullets smashed into them.

'It's an ambush! We've been sold out!' came Nelson's angry voice through their headsets.

The six men already had their own guns pointed in the direction of enemy gunfire, which was wild and haphazard, suggesting they weren't being attacked by trained soldiers. But bullets killed, no matter who was shooting.

Lying in a dip in the ground, behind a tree root,

Mitch scanned the area where most of the firing seemed to be coming from, on the other side of the clearing. It had been sheer good luck that the unit had run for the trees at this side. If they'd gone the other way, they'd have walked straight into the ambush.

How many of them? It was hard to tell.

'I've got a fix on the source of most of the machine guns,' came Two Moons' voice. 'I'm going to stick an RPG in the middle of them, see what shakes the tree.'

Two Moons already had the launcher ready, with the rocket-propelled grenade in place, poking out of the barrel. He levelled the rocket launcher and fired. It wasn't an easy shot, with trees and foliage on the other side of the clearing blocking the way, but Two Moons was an expert. There was an explosion from within the trees, a huge flash of fire, followed by screams.

'Hit 'em!' yelled Nelson.

While Two Moons reloaded the rocket launcher,

the other five soldiers poured tracers of bullets into the smoke where the RPG had struck. As men stumbled out of the jungle into the clearing, some with their clothes on fire or smouldering, the bullets cut them down.

More bullets hit the unit's position from other parts of the jungle.

'They're trying to come from the sides!' came Tug's voice. 'Troopers!'

Immediately Mitch switched a solid stream of gunfire to his left, while Gaz opened up to the unit's right. Benny continued laying down fire across the clearing into the trees opposite. Mitch could tell their shooting was having an effect by the fact that the firing from across the clearing had lessened.

'OK, let's take it to them!' Nelson said. 'Round the sides of the clearing. Mitch, you're with me. Gaz, you're with Tug. Benny and Two Moons, keep hitting them from here!'

Mitch followed Nelson as they began to work their way through the trees, heading towards the area at the left of the clearing. They crawled forward at speed, on hands and elbows, over tree roots and through gulleys, through shallow, swampy, stagnant mud that squelched and oozed and sucked at them. Tug and Gaz were doing the same on the other side. Meanwhile Benny kept up a steady stream of gunfire directly across the clearing, while Two Moons launched another two RPGs. More explosions, more screams, more smoke. It would create a diversion and give the four soldiers cover as they launched their counter-attack.

All Mitch's senses were alert as he scanned the shadowy trees ahead. Like Nelson, he kept low, his head popping up to check the area, each time in a different place and at a different angle, before ducking down again. Never give a marksman time to line your position up for a shot.

Suddenly Mitch saw them! Six men, moving forward, crouching, armed with machine guns and rifles. Nelson had seen them too. He nodded at Mitch, and both soldiers jumped up, fingers on their triggers, their streams of bullets tearing between the trees at their targets. Five of the six men crumpled to the ground. The sixth man swung his gun to aim at Nelson, but Mitch took him out with one burst.

There was the sound of rapid fire from their right, and then it fell silent. Benny and Two Moons had also stopped firing.

Mitch and Nelson waited, crouching behind the cover of the jungle trees, guns at the ready.

'OK,' said Nelson. 'Move forward, but keep under cover the whole way. Let's see what we've got. Watch out for tripwires.'

They moved forward slowly through the swampy jungle, every sense alert, ready for a sudden attack. But it didn't come. The final rustle of movement in the trees was the men of Delta Unit regrouping in an area scorched and devastated by Two Moons' rocket-launched grenades. Seven men lay dead around them.

'Seven here,' murmured Nelson. 'We caught six on the way, so that makes thirteen.'

'We took out eight,' said Tug.

'Twenty-one accounted for,' said Nelson thoughtfully. 'What do you think, Mitch? That all of them?'

Mitch shook his head. 'Depends who they are, but from my experience gangs here going out to attack tend to be bigger. Thirty at least.'

'The satellite pictures only showed twenty with Mwanga,' pointed out Benny.

'That's after they got him,' said Mitch. 'After the event they usually split into smaller groups.'

'So at least nine managed to get away,' said Nelson. 'Maybe more.' He turned to the unit. 'OK, guys, we all knows what this means, but I'm going to spell it out all the same. We were betrayed. This lot knew we were coming, and when and where. It may be nothing to do with Mwanga. For all we know they didn't learn the real reason we were coming in but decided to get rid of us because we got in their way. Or someone does know why we're really here and is set on stopping us. The bottom line is we're exposed. From now on we are a definite target. And we can't trust anyone. It could have been our chopper pilot who gave our position away, so we can't risk calling up a chopper to get out. We can't risk calling up *anyone*.

'So, we go on with the mission: we find Mwanga, and then we take him somewhere safe where we can get away, out of the Delta, but we do it on our own terms.'

'Mwanga may already be dead,' said Mitch.

'Or this attack may be proof he's still alive,' said Tug. He gestured at the dead bodies. 'If these men were part of the crowd who've got him, they could have been the first line of defence.'

'Maybe,' agreed Nelson. 'The thing is we don't know. Only one way to find out. We go on.'

'What do we do with them?' asked Benny, pointing at the dead bodies.

Nelson shrugged. 'Leave them,' he said. 'The jungle animals will take them soon enough. We move on.'

6

The jungle was thick and dark, and the men found themselves sinking into wet soil sometimes up to their knees if they strayed from the rough tracks made by animals.

They were travelling in single file, Nelson and Tug at the front, with Benny bringing up the rear. Gaz, Two Moons and Mitch were in the middle. Every man had his rifle at the ready in case of another ambush.

The air was so hot and humid that every movement covered the men with sweat, which attracted insects that clung to their skin.

'Is it always like this here?' asked Two Moons.

Mitch grinned. 'It never drops below sixty per cent humidity and sometimes goes right up to one hundred per cent. Think yourself lucky we're here in the dry season.'

'This is the dry season?' queried Two Moons.

Gaz laughed. 'Mitch is right,' he said. 'I did a couple of tours of duty in West Africa. Not in Nigeria, but in nearby countries. It's much the same there. Stinking hot and the air is just steam.'

'How long's this dry season last?' asked Two Moons.

'Two months,' answered Mitch. 'January and now, February. Once the rain kicks in, this jungle becomes a proper swamp. Then we'd be wading through it, up to our waists in water – and that's when the mosquitoes really come out and attack you.'

They saw that Tug, ahead of them, had stopped and thrown up his hand in the signal to freeze. They all stood and listened.

The sounds of the jungle were all around them: insects clicking, birds calling and fluttering through the leaves. Then they heard what Tug had heard: a heavier sound, something crashing through the leaves of the canopy above their heads.

'Monkeys,' said Mitch.

'Do they bite?' asked Two Moons.

'Only if you attack them,' replied Mitch.

'My cousin got bitten by a monkey,' said Gaz. 'He got infected and lost his arm.'

'Where was that?' asked Two Moons. 'One of these other West African countries you were talking about?'

Gaz shook his head. 'A zoo. He stuck his hand through the bars. He was an idiot.'

Suddenly the crashing sound got louder, and five monkeys passed above them, swinging from branch to branch, calling loudly to one another. Then they were gone.

Nelson signalled for the unit to move forward.

Mitch, just behind Tug and Nelson, heard the two commanders talking tactics.

'It's slow travelling through this jungle,' said Tug. 'If we travelled on open ground, we could get to the target quicker.'

'I thought of that, Tug,' said Nelson. 'But that ambush worries me. If they knew we were coming, the rest of the group will be watching out for us. Out in open ground we're an easy target for them. At least in the jungle they've got to come in and find us, and we'll hear them coming. Yeah, it's slower, but at least we've got more chance of staying alive.'

'But does Mwanga?' asked Tug. 'The longer they've got him, the more chance there is of them killing him.'

'Maybe,' said Nelson. 'We'll just have to wait and see.'

It was hard work but they made good time through the terrain, despite the difficult conditions. Every now and then they stopped when they heard a heavier noise than usual, but on each occasion it turned out to be an animal rooting in the swamp, or monkeys up in the high branches. Now and then a snake slithered by, or they saw the flicker of something vanishing into the undergrowth, but mostly their journey went without a hitch. The nearest they came to real danger was when Two Moons found himself sinking fast into a pit of oozing mud and the others had to pull him out without sinking in themselves.

'How deep is this mud?' asked Two Moons after they'd dragged him out of it.

'Depends,' replied Mitch. 'In some places, just waist deep. In others, you can sink right in over your head and disappear. The trouble is once you start sinking a vacuum forms under you that sucks you down more and more. Also, make sure no leeches get stuck to you. They can get in between any gaps in your clothing and they just love the taste of blood from nice warm moist skin.'

'I *have* been in jungle before,' said Two Moons.

'Yeah, but trust me, until you've been bitten by one of these leeches, you ain't been bitten,' finished Mitch.

They took turns to take the lead and to bring up the rear, and for part of the trek Mitch found himself guarding the rear with Tug. Unlike the others, Tug stayed silent. Mitch still wasn't sure whether this was just Tug's character or if Tug was still suspicious of him. At least Benny had put his opinion into words. Tug just stayed close-mouthed, his ears and eyes alert as they made their way through the jungle.

They had been travelling for about two hours when suddenly from about a mile ahead they heard the ear-splitting sound of automatic gunfire, followed by screaming and wailing.

7

The unit moved forward, rifles ready, crouching low, using the jungle as cover. Nelson was in front, Benny, Gaz and Tug watched the sides while Mitch and Two Moons guarded the rear, all alert for any sudden movements from the jungle around them. All the time the sound of terrified wailing was getting nearer.

They reached a point where the jungle ended and saw a small village: a collection of mud huts with roofs made of palm branches, and some dwellings made from bits of corrugated iron and plastic.

Two men sat on a battered open jeep. Both of them carried automatic rifles, which they held casually across their laps.

Another armed man was standing in the clearing

at the centre of the village, aiming his rifle at a group of women and children.

Further back stood a couple of unarmed men, both with their hands on top of their heads. Two more armed men covered them with rifles.

But all the unit's attention was drawn to the sixth man, the obvious leader of the gang. A golden headband was tied round his shaven skull, and he was more heavily armed than the rest. As well as an automatic rifle slung over his back, he had loaded ammunition belts hanging from his shoulders, and a vicious-looking machete in his right hand. With his left hand he was gripping the hair of a man kneeling in front of him and he was shouting at the man. Specks of spittle came from his mouth as he yelled and waved the machete menacingly.

The kneeling man said nothing, but Mitch could see blood trickling from his mouth and nose.

'Any idea what's going on?' Nelson whispered to Mitch.

'A raiding party,' murmured Mitch. 'Looks like

some local warlord and his gang. Rob, loot and terrify. It's an occupational hazard here.'

'Think they could be rebels?' asked Nelson. 'You know, part of the group holding Mwanga?'

'Could be,' replied Mitch. 'But they could just as easily be a bunch of regular bandits grabbing what they can.'

'I say we leave them alone and move on,' said Benny. 'It's a local issue. We've got a mission to complete. We get involved here, it blows our cover. Plus, we could take casualties, and it's the wrong time for that. We need every man we've got if we're going to free Mwanga.'

Nelson said nothing, just kept his eyes on what was happening in the village.

The bandits watched their leader. From the grins on their faces it was obvious they were enjoying what was happening.

'Seems to me our cover's blown anyway,' put in Two Moons. 'Otherwise we wouldn't have been shot at as soon as we arrived.'

'You think we ought to intervene, Two Moons?' asked Nelson.

Two Moons nodded. 'I hate bullies,' he said. 'We let 'em get away with this, they'll keep coming back. Keep terrorising these villagers. And my guess is that fella with the gold headband sure ain't gonna use that machete for cleaning his fingernails.'

'This is not part of our mission,' insisted Benny. 'We screw up here, who's going to rescue Mwanga?'

'I agree with Benny,' put in Tug. 'I'm sympathetic to the plight of these people, but we have a mission. That's why we're here, and we mustn't jeopardise that.'

'What about you other guys?' Nelson asked Mitch and Gaz.

'I'm with Two Moons,' said Gaz.

'Me too,' said Mitch. 'For one thing, these bandits are in our way. They could be a problem when we're coming back with Mwanga. If we take 'em out now, that's one less obstacle for us to deal with later.'

Nelson nodded. 'Three to two, gentlemen,' he murmured to Benny and Tug.

'You're the commanding officer,' Tug pointed out to him.

'Damn right,' agreed Nelson. 'Which gives me two votes. So, it's five to two on us going in.' He grinned. 'I *really* don't like that gold headband he's wearing.'

The leader had now raised the machete above his head and was waving it around threateningly. The man kneeling on the ground closed his eyes and tried to push his head into his shoulders, as if it would stop him being attacked.

'If we're going to move, we'd better move fast,' said Gaz. 'Before he chops that guy's head off.'

'He's not going to chop his head off,' said Mitch. 'If he does that, the village packs up and moves on, which means no more stealing from them in the future.'

'So it's going to be OK,' said Tug. 'He's not going to kill him. Just threaten him.'

Mitch shook his head. 'No. He'll cut one of the

man's hands off, as an example to the others. Then he'll start on the others. Cut a hand off one of the women or one or two of the kids.'

'When?' asked Benny.

'Any second now,' said Mitch.

As they watched, the leader let go of the kneeling man's hair, grabbed the man's left hand and pulled it out from his side. The women began to scream as the machete was swung back.

Bang! In one movement Nelson had brought his rifle up to his shoulder, switched it to single shot, and fired. The bullet took the leader right through the head, and he fell sideways, eyes wide in surprise.

The two men sitting on the jeep gaped, stunned at the sight of their leader's body tumbling heavily to the ground. Then they sprang into action, rifles leaping into their hands. But the unit was already moving.

A spray of automatic fire from Two Moons and Gaz took out the other two men near the jeep.

'Save the hostages!' shouted Nelson.

Mitch, Benny and Tug were already running towards the village men standing with their hands on their heads, now looking terrified. The two armed bandits by them hesitated, still shocked by what had happened to their leader.

Benny let fly a hail of bullets and one of the bandits crumpled to the ground. The other bandit turned and began to run.

Bang!

A burst of fire from Tug took the fleeing bandit's legs from under him and he crashed to the ground, screaming with pain.

'We've got one prisoner at least,' grunted Tug.

'I wouldn't count on it,' murmured Mitch.

As the unit watched, they realised the women had broken away from their previous position and were running towards the wounded bandit. As they ran, they gathered up their farming tools: axes, picks, shovels and rakes. They were still shouting and wailing, but these were now screams

61

of triumph and revenge, not of fear.

'They're going to kill him?' asked Gaz.

'That's the general idea,' said Mitch.

'We have to stop them!' said Tug, and he fired a burst of gunfire into the air.

The running women stopped, hesitated, then carried on.

'Do something!' snapped Tug. 'You know the language, Mitch. Shout at them! Tell them to stop!'

'Why?' Mitch shrugged. 'These bandits will have been living off the people of this village like parasites for ages. Looting, torturing, murdering.'

As he spoke, the women had reached the fallen bandit and had begun striking him with their farm implements. The bandit's screams ceased.

'You stupid idiot!' Tug raged angrily at Mitch. 'We could have got some intel from that prisoner! Information about the rebels. Now he's dead we won't find out anything!'

'Yes, we will,' said Mitch calmly. 'And a lot quicker and more truthfully.' He gestured at the villagers, who were now approaching them, slowly and warily, but with their hands held out in a gesture of peace and with smiles of gratitude on their faces. 'We've just made ourselves some new and very useful friends.'

8

While the men of the village and the rest of the unit disposed of the bandits' bodies, Mitch and Nelson sat down to talk to the leader of the village. His name, he told them, was Adwana, and these bandits had been terrorising his village for a very long time. At least, that was the impression Nelson got from the gestures Adwana made with his arms and hands, stretching them out to show a long length of time, accompanied by the clicking noises and almost singsong rhythms of the native language.

'You understand all this?' Nelson asked Mitch.

'Most of it,' replied Mitch. He turned back to Adwana. 'We're here to help Joseph Mwanga,' he said, using the same mixture of tonal sounds and clicks.

Adwana nodded. 'We heard there were strangers coming to save Mwanga,' he told Mitch. 'The bandits said so.' Adwana spat on the ground to show his disgust at the word 'bandits'. 'They wanted to know if we had seen anyone dressed like you. Like soldiers. American. British.'

So they did know we were coming, thought Mitch.

Mitch and Adwana talked while Nelson listened. Nelson hadn't a clue what either man was saying, but he could tell by the body language, the way they were using their hands to explain themselves, that the conversation was going well. Adwana was keen to give as much help as he could to the men who had saved his hand, and his people.

At one point Adwana turned and called another man over. Nelson gathered that this man was called Oba, and soon Mitch, Adwana and Oba were engaged in a three-way conversation that went on for some time. Mitch gently asked questions, listening and nodding as Adwana and Oba replied.

A couple of times Nelson noticed that Mitch seemed puzzled by an answer, and when that happened he frowned and repeated what either Adwana or Oba had said, with a few additional questioning words in Igbo himself, until he had made sure he'd understood the answer correctly. Then, Mitch would smile, nod and move on.

By the time Mitch seemed satisfied, and the conversation had ended with smiles and handshakes all round, the light was fading.

Nelson smelt food cooking, and noticed that the women of the village were preparing something in a pot over a fire.

'Let me guess,' he said. 'It's supper time.'

Mitch nodded. 'And we're the honoured guests.' As Mitch saw Nelson's eyes stray to his watch and his mouth open to argue, Mitch added hastily: 'It would be rude to refuse. Eating with an invited guest is very important to these people. We'll be seriously insulting them if we leave now – and we need their help.'

Nelson hesitated, then nodded.

The sounds of the other village men and soldiers approaching made them look up.

'All tidied up,' said Tug. 'We can move on.'

'It seems we can't,' said Nelson. 'Local tradition says we have to eat.'

Two Moons grinned. 'No argument from me,' he said. 'That food smells great. A lot better than our emergency rations.'

'What have they told you?' Benny asked Nelson.

Nelson jerked his thumb at Mitch. 'I'm hoping that's what Mitch is going to tell us while we eat,' he said. 'And I hope they ain't just been talking about the weather and crops.'

By now night had fallen. As always in the tropics, it happened quickly. One moment it was daylight, the next, following a very brief period that could have been described as dusk, it was dark.

The men of Delta Unit joined the villagers sitting on the ground near the fires that sent showers of sparks into the dark sky, and on which the food was cooking.

Benny picked a piece of food from his wooden bowl and sniffed it, before popping it into his mouth.

'Smoked fish,' he said. 'It's good.'

'It's what everyone here eats,' Mitch told him. 'That, and monkey meat.'

'Mitch, can we move on from this gourmet-chef stuff and get on with what these guys told you?' asked Nelson, a touch of impatience in his tone.

Mitch nodded. 'The group holding Mwanga is led by a warlord called Justis Ngola,' he said. 'For good measure, it just so happens that the bandit chief with the gold headband we just took out is a cousin of this same Justis Ngola.'

'So this is a family business,' commented Tug.

'Do they know why Mwanga was kidnapped in the first place?' asked Benny.

'The word is that someone very important paid Justis Ngola a lot of money to have Mwanga captured and killed.'

'So Mwanga's dead?' asked Gaz ruefully.

Mitch shook his head. 'No. According to Adwana, Mwanga is still alive and being kept hostage by Ngola and his men.'

'Why?' asked Tug. 'If this Ngola was paid to kill Mwanga, whoever paid him is either going to start looking for revenge, or his money back.'

'Ngola's only been paid half the money. He gets the balance when Mwanga is found dead. But, like many criminals, Ngola is hoping to make a bit more out of it. He's realised what a special commodity he's got on his hands, so he's upped the price to the original buyer, and at the same time he's planning to see if anyone else will offer a better price. In the end, the highest bidder gets Mwanga. Alive, if they want him that way, or dead. It makes no difference to Ngola. But he'll only hand over the goods once he's been paid the money.'

'Do these people know where Ngola is holding Mwanga?'

'Adwana says it's a big place where people stay. It

sounds like it used to be a hotel of some sorts. Now it's been taken over by Ngola as his headquarters. It's about ten miles away from here. According to the villagers, Ngola has turned it into a fortress.'

'OK.' Benny sat back. 'So we've got what we want.'

'We've got better than that,' grinned Mitch. He gestured at Oba who was now sitting near them, watching the soldiers as he ate his meal. 'Oba here says he'll take us to the place.'

'Can we trust him?' asked Tug. 'He could be leading us into a trap. He could be getting a handsome pay-off if he betrays us to the rebels.'

'I'm with Tug,' agreed Benny. 'These people have given us information – surely that's enough. Why put themselves at real risk by siding with us against the rebels? If he's caught, the village will suffer even more than it already has.'

'Oba's wife and his brother were killed by those bandits,' explained Mitch. 'He says he wants to show his thanks to us for killing them. Plus, our friend,

Gold Headband, was from the same tribe as the rebels,' replied Mitch. 'These people are a different tribe. The tribal thing is very big here.'

'It's big everywhere,' said Two Moons. 'Rival gangs in Los Angeles, New York.'

'Newcastle, Liverpool,' agreed Gaz. 'Different people, same problem.'

'OK,' said Nelson. 'We take up Oba's very kind offer. Let's eat up and go.'

Mitch held up his hand. 'We don't go that quickly,' he said. 'Adwana and Oba say it's bad magic to go through the jungle at night. Hungry animals are there. Lots of places to sink in swamps.'

'So? Tell him we've got night-vision goggles,' said Nelson. 'Tell him we do some of our best work at night.'

'We might, he doesn't,' said Mitch.

'He could borrow a night-vision set,' suggested Gaz. 'I've got a spare in my pack.'

Mitch shook his head. 'It's more than that,' he said. 'It's about the bad magic.'

The others exchanged thoughtful looks. They all knew how important local customs were. If you wanted to win the hearts and minds of local people, you respected their customs and traditions.

Nelson nodded. 'OK,' he said. 'So when is good for us to go?'

Mitch turned to Oba and asked him a question. Oba replied, and Mitch turned to the others.

'First thing tomorrow morning, just before dawn. Oba says the magic isn't so strong then, even though it's still dark. Let's face it, that jungle was difficult enough terrain during daylight hours. At night, even with night vision, the chances of us sinking in mud or getting stuck are pretty high.'

Nelson thought it over, and then agreed.

'OK,' he said. 'It'll give us time to check our equipment, and grab a bit of shut-eye.' He checked his watch. 'Turn and turn about: three sleep, three on watch. Gaz, Tug and Benny, you three grab some sleep first. I'll take first watch with Mitch and Two Moons.'

9

Mitch and Two Moons sat back to back at the edge of the village so they could keep watch on a full 360 degrees, taking in the village and the jungle. Nelson was on his own, patrolling the perimeter, rifle at the ready. The village was quiet. Everyone else was asleep. The fires had burnt down and now only ash glowed red amongst the grey of the embers in the cooking pits.

Around them, the jungle resonated with the sounds of the night animals: chitter chattering, slithering and an occasional howling.

'Guess those are the bad spirits out there,' murmured Two Moons.

'Guess so,' said Mitch.

Two Moons shook his head and said, 'Here we

are, with gizmos to get us through any situation, and we take advice about not going through the jungle at night from a guy who believes in magic.'

'I wouldn't have thought you'd have a problem with that,' responded Mitch, with a wry smile. 'When I was in Arizona I met a whole bunch of Native Americans talking about being guided by spirits.'

'That's different,' said Two Moons. 'Our beliefs don't stop us using modern things. Some of our people believe we should only ride horses and use bows and arrows to hunt, because that's what our ancestors did. Me, I can chase a buffalo faster in a jeep than I can on a horse and I can shoot it quicker and cleaner with a rifle.'

'You hunt buffalo?' asked Mitch, impressed.

'Well, no,' admitted Two Moons. 'I prefer a good beef burger. But if I was going to hunt, I'd use a rifle and four wheels. Each to their own.'

'If you think about it, Adwana's belief in magic is no different to a modern army being given a blessing by a priest before they go into battle.' Mitch shrugged. 'It's just a different sort of magic, that's all.'

'You don't believe in magic, Mitch?' asked Two Moons. 'You don't believe in any sort of religion?'

Mitch grinned. 'I believe in *everything*,' he said. 'I'm taking no chances. When I get to heaven, it doesn't matter what sort of God or juju is there waiting for me, I'm gonna be OK.'

'You're just an opportunistic cynic,' said Two Moons.

'Absolutely,' agreed Mitch. 'And it's kept me alive so far, so I'm hardly likely to change now.'

Silence descended between them, and they sat there, listening, ears strained for any sounds other than the background noise of the jungle: a metallic click, a boot on brush.

They watched Nelson as he patrolled, eyes and ears always alert.

Two Moons broke the silence: 'Don't come down too hard on Tug.'

'I didn't think I was,' said Mitch.

'It's in your eyes,' said Two Moons. 'You don't like him.'

'It's not a case of liking him or not,' said Mitch. 'He makes it pretty clear he's suspicious of me. But that's OK.'

'I'm talking about this business of him not trusting the villagers. He had a bad experience. He was with a unit in Afghanistan that took the word of some locals. The locals sold 'em out. Tug was the only one that survived. Since then he don't trust nobody, 'cept us in Delta Unit.'

'Which doesn't include me,' said Mitch.

'Not yet,' said Two Moons. 'Give him time.'

'You guys been together long?'

Two Moons nodded. 'Nearly two years, which – in this business – is a long while for a bunch of guys to stay together as one unit.'

'What happened to the guy I replaced?' asked Mitch.

Two Moons shrugged. 'Joe McNeil,' he said. 'He

died. He was trying to defuse a bomb. The bastard who rigged it had booby-trapped it.' He gave a wry sigh. 'I liked Joe. We all did. He used to make us laugh.'

'We all lose people in this game,' said Mitch. 'It's the way we live. Doesn't matter how on the ball we are, we're always on the edge and one breath away from dying.'

Two Moons laughed. 'When you say it like that, it sure is a hell of a stupid way to earn a living.'

10

They woke before dawn the next morning, refreshed. Nelson gestured at the bandits' jeep. 'They'd better not leave that sitting around,' he commented to Mitch. 'If the bad guys show up and see it, this village will be in real big trouble.'

'I was just thinking the same,' agreed Mitch. He called Adwana over and passed on Nelson's advice about getting rid of the jeep, with a few extra tips of his own.

'What did you tell him?' asked Nelson after he'd finished.

'Told him to take it out into the jungle and abandon it as far away as possible. If he can, find a ravine to run it into.'

'Good,' said Nelson.

The unit gathered up their gear, then set off for the bandit stronghold, with Oba leading the way.

As Mitch had said, with a guide like Oba who knew the jungle like the back of his hand, they covered the ten miles in five hours. On difficult terrain like this, with swamps and deep gulleys to get across, it was fast going.

Suddenly Oba began to slow down and then stopped, his eyes darting around, obviously afraid. The confidence with which he had moved through the jungle suddenly vanished.

'I think we're here,' Mitch murmured to the others.

He whispered something to Oba in Igbo, and Oba nodded, pointing ahead. As gently and as calmly as he could, Mitch talked to Oba, gesturing at the other men of Delta Unit, and assuring Oba that no harm would come to him while they were with him.

Oba nodded slowly, but it was obvious from his face and his body language that he wasn't convinced. However, he dropped down on to his hands and knees and began crawling slowly forward through the jungle. Delta Unit dropped down too, and followed him.

It took ten minutes of slow and careful crawling through the tangle of bush and tree roots, but at last they could see a huge clearing in the jungle. The clearing was covered in overgrown foliage from ornamental plants and bushes, small trees and shrubs that had once been cultivated and kept neat and tidy, but had now grown wild. Rising up from the rampant vegetation was a dilapidated two-storey-high concrete building. The remains of a tennis court could be seen through the trees, as well as the cracked tiles and empty shell of what had once been a large swimming pool. A faded broken sign hanging on the wall near the main entrance announced it was the 'Malinawi Hotel'.

'Nice place to come for a holiday,' commented Gaz.

The place had obviously been built for better

times, in the hope that tourists would come out with their dollars and pounds and bring luxury to the area. Either the tourists hadn't materialised, or the developer had run out of cash before the place could be completed. Or maybe a civil war had just overtaken the place. Now, the hotel looked like a makeshift fortress. The windows had been boarded up, sheets of wood and corrugated iron nailed into place over them.

'Making sure no one throws any grenades into the building,' murmured Benny.

The grounds were patrolled by guards, all dressed raggedly and as casually as the other crew of bandits had been. But they were all heavily armed, bandoliers of ammunition hanging from their shoulders, assault rifles dangling from their hands.

Nelson and Tug scanned the building and the armed men through their binoculars.

'How many can you make out?' asked Nelson.

'Ten,' muttered Tug. 'And that's only from this side. My guess is there'll be at least another ten out of sight on the other side.'

'That's what I'm thinking,' agreed Nelson. 'So, twenty outside. How many inside? What d'you think, Mitch?'

Mitch shrugged. 'Hard to tell,' he said. 'Ten, twenty. It depends if they've got any of their men out on patrol.'

They studied the men outside the hotel. Most of them seemed very relaxed, joking and laughing with one another, but a few stalked around, guns levelled. They carried a mixture of weapons. Some had AK-47s, one or two had Steyr AUGs and a couple were carrying SKS semi-automatic rifles. One thing was sure: all the weapons had deadly firepower, even in amateur hands.

'Considering they're supposed to know we're here, they don't seem very bothered,' commented Two Moons.

'They don't know we've got this far yet,' whispered Tug.

'And this isn't an army,' added Mitch. 'This is

just a bunch of gung-ho trigger-happy bandits. My guess is they think they're safe here. Look at the building. There's no sign of any damage to it from weapons. No burn marks. No shell damage.'

'There are bullet holes in the walls,' pointed out Gaz.

'Target practice when they're feeling bored,' suggested Nelson.

'This place has never been attacked,' agreed Mitch. 'Why should it be? Locals wouldn't attack it because they're too scared of this Ngola. Just take a look at Oba.'

Oba was crouched low, his eyes darting from the derelict hotel to the armed men.

Nelson turned to Mitch. 'Ask him if he knows the layout inside this place.'

Mitch nodded and asked Oba if he or anyone he knew had ever been inside the building. Oba's answer brought a smile to Mitch's face.

'We're in luck,' he told the others. 'Oba worked here for a while years ago when he was a kid, when the place was a working hotel. He was a cleaner.'

Taking a sheet of paper and a pencil, Mitch persuaded Oba to draw a rough plan of the hotel to show where the various rooms were: the bedrooms, the kitchen, the dining room, the toilets. All the time he was drawing the sketch plan, Oba kept throwing nervous glances towards the building and the armed bandits.

'He's terrified,' said Two Moons.

'I don't blame him,' said Gaz. 'We know what these people can do.'

Mitch tried to calm Oba down, assuring him that the questions would only take a little longer, but it soon became obvious that Oba's fear of Justis Ngola and his gang was overwhelming. He looked more and more towards the building and the armed men patrolling outside. Mitch was finding it harder to keep his attention.

'We'd better let him go,' Mitch said to Nelson. 'We don't want him suddenly freaking out and doing something that draws attention to us. He's been brave enough to bring us here, and he's given us a plan of the inside of the place. I think he's done enough.'

'Agreed,' said Nelson, nodding.

He smiled at Oba and held out his hand to the man. Oba didn't take it – his attention was now focused entirely on the wrecked hotel. In a quiet voice, Mitch thanked Oba and told him he was free to go. Oba gratefully slipped back into the jungle and had soon disappeared from view.

Mitch handed the sketch plan of the hotel to Nelson, who studied it.

'Good work,' Nelson said. 'Some of this may have changed, of course.'

'True,' said Mitch, 'but even if they're using the rooms differently my guess is the walls will still be in place.' He tapped the sketch map. 'There's a basement. I bet that's where they'll be holding Mwanga.'

'Makes sense.' Tug nodded in agreement. 'More secure.'

Nelson folded the sheet of paper up and tucked it into his pocket. 'Now to scout the place out,' he said. 'See where the weak points are. We need to confirm that Mwanga is in the basement. We need to see if we can work out how many men are in this place, and where they are. Make sure we know the location of all the entrances and exits. Any windows that look like they can be opened up. Possible traps. Everything we can.

'Mitch and Tug, you're with me. Gaz and Two Moons, you're with Benny. Get as much intel as you can about the place. Meet back here in thirty minutes.'

Mitch and Tug followed Nelson to the east. Two Moons, Gaz and Benny headed west, all of them crouching low and keeping to the cover of the jungle.

A motley collection of vehicles was scattered outside the front of the building: six off-road cars, a battered ambulance and two lorries, including one with the words 'Food Charity' stencilled on the side.

'Hijacked vehicles,' muttered Tug.

He produced a small digital camera and began taking photos of the building every ten metres or so to get shots from different angles. Memory could play tricks; a photo was hard evidence.

Doing the recce was slow work. Fast movements could catch the eye of anybody watching and it was crucial not to rustle branches and disturb things, both plants and animals. Scare a bird and it would give away your position. So the men moved forward on their hands and knees, bellies sliding over the uneven ground, stopping for a minute at each vantage point before moving on, aware all the time of the armed men patrolling just a short distance away.

Nelson, Tug and Mitch crawled along until they came to a dust track that cut through the jungle to the hotel. The lack of weeds and the many tyre tracks showed the road was still in constant use.

So far they had scouted two sides of the hotel.

The third side faced away from them, and to get to that they'd have to cross the road. Mitch gestured at the jungle on the other side of the road.

Nelson shook his head. 'Too risky. We don't want to get spotted this early. The road's a dead end, so the other guys should be able to check out that side from their direction.' He checked his watch. 'We'll head back and wait for them.'

The three men retraced their steps, using the same 'crawl and stop' routine as before. They got back to the rendezvous point first. Benny, Two Moons and Gaz joined them five minutes afterwards. They moved deeper into the jungle to avoid detection and swapped observations.

'Fifteen men outside at different places,' summed up Nelson. 'Ten at the front, five at the back, but they keep moving around, exchanging positions.'

'The good thing is there's lots of cover because of all the overgrown vegetation,' said Tug.

'And it goes right up to the walls of the building,' added Benny. 'Plus there are the old outbuildings for the tennis courts, and storage sheds. All offer good cover.'

'The question is: how many men are we dealing with?' asked Tug. 'How many are inside the building?'

'The villagers said they reckoned about thirty men are here,' said Mitch. 'That makes sense, if you think about it. The satellite showed twenty men with Mwanga. Add another ten who stay and keep guard on the place when the raiding party is away and that gives us our thirty. So, we saw fifteen outside, and although some men may be out on patrol I think we should assume at least fifteen inside.'

'OK, let's look at ways into the building,' said Nelson. 'We saw the main entrance and two smaller doors round the side. The doors to the main entrance looked open, but there are at least two armed guards just inside them. The two smaller doors were shut, but whether they're locked, and how thick the doors are, we don't know. What did you see, Benny?'

Benny shook his head. 'Two small doors at the back. Both shut, could be locked. No windows easily accessible. The downstairs ones are all very tightly secured with sheets of corrugated iron. Wood's been used to board up the windows on the upper floor.'

'It looks like the building's power comes from a generator,' said Gaz. 'There's an outbuilding with an oil tank next to it on the far side.'

Nelson nodded thoughtfully, taking all this in.

'We really need more intel on what's going on inside,' he said. 'Where Mwanga is. Where Justis Ngola is inside the building. Where the other fifteen men are. We need to get the intel and set up a proper plan of attack, and then we go in as soon as it gets dark. They've got a numbers advantage, but we've got night vision. If we take out the generator that provides electricity just before we go in, it'll be pitch black inside there. That makes it almost a level playing field.'

'I'm thinking the longer we wait the more chance there is we'll find Mwanga dead,' put in Tug.

'I don't think so,' disagreed Mitch. 'Mwanga's their pay cheque. OK, one side wants him dead, but it's looking like someone equally rich wants him alive. Justis Ngola will want to keep Mwanga alive until the money arrives.'

'Makes sense to me,' said Nelson. 'So, the plan is we split up again and do a full recce. See what intel we can get. Then, tonight, we take out the generator and go in. Right now, three teams of two spread out to watch the place. Me with Tug, Benny with Two Moons, Gaz with Mitch. Stay in radio contact, but keep it to a minimum. Let's not alert the opposition. OK?'

11

The first thing Mitch and Gaz did when they reached their observation point was make a hide for themselves. They chose a spot just inside the jungle, but with a clear view of the hotel through the trees and bushes.

They found a dip in the jungle floor and dug and scraped away at it until they had created a shallow trench, large enough for the two of them to lie down. Then they covered it with branches to make a roof, and overlaid that with big leaves and brush. They knew that the other two teams would be doing the same at their vantage points, covering the bandits' HQ from three positions, which would give them an overall view of the whole place.

As Mitch and Gaz settled down under their hide,

Mitch reflected that during his time in Special Forces he'd spent more time carrying out observation than he had in actual combat. Gathering intelligence was what kept him alive. You had to know where the enemy was, and how many you were up against. What weapons did they have? If they were in a building, was the building booby-trapped? Which were the fastest ways in and out of it?

If the mission was to rescue hostages, you had to know where the hostages were being kept. Were they together or separate? How many guards were with them? Were they inexperienced and trigger-happy, or more cautious?

'What's the longest observation you've done, Gaz?' asked Mitch.

Gaz thought about it. 'Three weeks,' he said. 'Sitting in a hole in the desert watching a border and waiting for some terrorists to come over.'

'Did they come?'

Gaz nodded. 'Problem was they came over the day after we were pulled out.'

'So your position had been betrayed?'

Again, Gaz nodded. 'That's the way it looked to me afterwards. It's often struck me that it's a crazy situation: the enemy tries to kill you, and the people on your side betray you. You and me and the others have got to be mad to be doing this.'

'Of course we are,' agreed Mitch. 'That's why we like doing it.'

Gaz laughed. 'True,' he agreed. Then suddenly something at the hotel caught his eye. He lifted his binoculars and looked hard at the building.

'What have you seen?' asked Mitch.

'One of the downstairs windows,' said Gaz. 'The corner of the sheet of iron has come loose. I didn't notice it before, but then I saw the shadow. It's bigger in that one corner than at the other corners.'

Mitch scanned the window through his own binoculars.

'I think you're right,' he said.

'If I am, then an observations gizmo would

94

serve us well. A camera would be good, but even a microphone should be able to pick things up.'

Mitch studied the side of the building. 'Getting there to put it in place could be a problem,' he said. 'There are ten armed men between us and the hotel building, remember?'

'There's enough cover,' said Gaz. 'Bushes, vehicles, outbuildings. I've done this with less cover and more guards around. Like you said, these guys aren't professionals. They're sloppy, which helps us.'

'I've nearly been caught out by sloppy guards before,' said Mitch. 'I was hiding in a ditch once, keeping observation on a building, when this guy came out for a pee and actually pissed on me. If he'd looked more closely at what he was doing, I'd have been caught for sure.'

Gaz grinned. 'I'll watch out for anyone taking a leak,' he said. He triggered his headset intercom, giving the call sign, and they heard Nelson's voice. Using as few words as possible, Gaz outlined the proposal for him to get to the window and plant a listening and viewing device at the exposed corner of the downstairs window.

There was a brief muttered discussion between Nelson and Tug, and then Nelson's voice said: 'We're thinking the same on this side. We reckon we can get a mic in place. So go. But if it looks sticky, abort. We don't blow this.'

Gaz clicked off his intercom and then pulled a roll of cloth out of his pack, which he opened to reveal an array of tiny transmitters and cameras.

'Were you a private eye before you came into this?' asked Mitch, impressed.

Gaz shook his head. 'No, I was a burglar. These things saved me from getting caught. Well, not these *exact* things, but earlier versions.'

'How long were you a burglar for?' asked Mitch, surprised and intrigued.

'From the time I was ten until I was sixteen. I worked with my Uncle George. He showed me the ropes,' explained Gaz.

'So what made you join the army?'

'Uncle George robbed some big-time gangster in Gateshead who took offence and had him killed. I had to disappear before he worked out I was in on it, so I joined the army.' He shrugged. 'Burglary taught me a few useful skills, but it's not a part of my past I'm proud of, and it's not something I'd ever go back to. I hated doing it. But hey, you live and learn.'

Gaz had selected a small piece of apparatus and tucked it into his top pocket. Then he handed something to Mitch. It looked like a mobile phone, complete with a small screen.

'This the receiver?' asked Mitch.

Gaz nodded. 'I've set the frequencies so it should start picking up as soon as I've got it in place.'

Mitch lay down near the edge of the clearing and trained his rifle on the armed men hanging around outside the front of the hotel. He put the small mobile-phone-like receiver on the ground next to him so he could see the tiny screen.

'Let's keep radio silence,' Gaz said. 'Just in case

they've got sharp hearing.'

Mitch nodded in agreement. 'If any shooting starts, I'll come and get you,' he promised.

Gaz shook his head. 'No need,' he said. 'Just give me covering fire if it comes to that. I'll look after myself.'

With that, Gaz edged forward, crawling to the point where the jungle became the overgrown garden of the hotel.

12

Mitch watched as Gaz slid out towards the hotel.

On this side he could see six armed men keeping guard, but only one of them really seemed to be alert. Three of them were playing with dice, while two others sat on the fallen trunks of trees, their rifles held casually by their sides. The sixth stood up and paced around, jerking his rifle this way and that, aiming it into the jungle.

Mitch shifted his binoculars to follow Gaz's progress. As Gaz had said, there was lots of cover. But in a few places there were just open areas of grass. If Gaz was spotted moving across these open areas, the trigger-happy bandits would open fire and the operation would be blown. The firing would bring the rest of the bandits out of the hotel.

As Mitch weighed up the situation, he found himself fingering the trigger of his assault rifle, ready to swing into action. If anything went wrong, he was determined to do everything he could to make sure Gaz wasn't killed.

He kept switching his attention backwards and forwards between the armed bandits and Gaz.

Mitch prided himself on being able to move covertly, but as he watched Gaz, he had to admit that the Geordie was a real expert. Gaz seemed to slide from bush to bush, tree to tree, keeping flat, using no rapid movements, but at the same time progressing so swiftly that there was no time for anyone to get a fix on him. It was the nearest Mitch had ever come to seeing a human snake on the move.

Gaz reached the building without an alarm being raised and slid up to the window where the corrugated iron sheeting had come away at one corner. Slowly, Gaz rose up from the ground, his back against the wall, his eyes on the armed guards.

The guards were still in the same positions as before: one reasonably alert, with his assault rifle at the ready, three playing dice, two lounging around and chatting.

Gaz turned and began to prise the iron sheet apart, but as he did so Mitch saw one of the men suddenly stand up and raise his gun.

Gaz must have seen him too, because he dropped out of sight behind a shrub.

Had the man heard something? Seen a movement out of the corner of his eye?

Mitch moved the barrel of his rifle so that it was now aimed at the man who'd got up. His finger was poised on the trigger. To shoot now would blow the mission, but so would letting Gaz be captured.

The man who'd got up said something to the others, and then headed for the main entrance of the hotel. There was no urgency in his movements. Maybe he just wanted to get something to eat or drink.

Mitch's attention switched back to the window.

There was a pause as Gaz waited for the man to get inside the hotel entrance. Then he rose up slowly and quietly again. Mitch saw him push the transmitter in between the corrugated iron and the window, and then he dropped down out of sight.

Immediately the small receiver by Mitch's side began humming, and then voices could be heard coming from it. They were muffled, but if he strained hard to listen Mitch could pick up what was being said.

On the small screen Mitch could make out some movements, but nothing very clear – mainly just shadows in the background.

Mitch kept his eyes and his rifle on the building and the bandits, watching out for Gaz. He spotted the Geordie every now and then, surfacing from beneath a bush or from a dip in the ground, and then sliding on to another sheltered point.

Finally, Gaz made it back to the hide and Mitch. He gestured at the small receiver.

'Getting anything?' he asked.

Mitch nodded. 'Sound and vision working OK,' he confirmed. 'Now I guess we just wait, watch and listen.'

13

After some close observations using the transmitter, they heard Nelson radio with instructions for everyone to regroup at the original location.

'Looks like we're ready to roll,' muttered Gaz as he and Mitch gathered their weapons and headed back through the trees.

When they arrived, Two Moons and Benny were already there with Nelson and Tug. Nelson had drawn a more detailed plan of the hotel buildings and grounds, with extra information from what he and Tug, and Two Moons and Benny, had observed and picked up.

'We managed to get a mic and camera in a hole in the wall,' explained Two Moons.

'We did the same thing in one of the windows,'

said Mitch. Then he added with a grin, 'Or, to be fair, Gaz did. I just watched him.'

Quickly, Mitch and Gaz told the rest of the unit what they'd been able to pick up from their own observations.

'There are between five and six men on guard at the front as a general rule. Another three, all fully armed, roaming around the side. Now and then they join up with their pals at the front, and then go off and chat to their mates round the back of the hotel,' said Gaz. 'There was a change-over about an hour ago. Nothing organised, it all looked pretty casual. Some guys came out from inside, and some of the guys who were outside went in. But the numbers stayed pretty much the same.'

'What intel did you get from your mic and camera?' asked Nelson.

'It looks like that room at the front is some kind of eating place,' said Mitch. 'You can just make out a fridge in one corner. And there are cans and bottles. Lots of sounds of cans being opened. We picked up a flare that looks to me like a flame from a stove of some sort. From what we can see, the place inside is a dump. They cook, eat and drink without clearing up and throw their rubbish and their clothes on the floor.'

'Sounds like some of the places I used to live in Newcastle,' said Gaz, smiling.

Nelson added their information to the plan. Then, 'Do we know if Justis Ngola is actually in the building?' he asked. 'Or are we just watching a bunch of second-grade bandits hanging around?'

'We think he is,' said Benny. 'We couldn't work out what was being said, but there's one voice that sounds like it's giving orders.'

'How can you be sure?' asked Gaz. 'Could just be someone drunk and lairy.'

'No one talks back to him, though,' said Two Moons. 'They all shut up when he speaks.'

'Might be a good idea if Mitch took a listen to it,' said Nelson. 'See if he can make anything out.'

Benny handed the receiver over to Mitch.

'This is it,' he said.

Mitch took the small machine and began to listen, making notes on a pad. Now and then one voice stood out, clearer and louder than the others. As Two Moons had said, when this voice spoke there were only muted responses and no one seemed to argue with him.

'That sounds like the boss, all right,' said Mitch. 'He's telling the others what to do. It also sounds like he's getting phone calls now and then, so I guess he's got a satellite phone. That'd be the only way he'd get a signal in this jungle. When he got a call just now, he shouted and said: "I don't care about that. Where's the money?" At one point he yelled, "If I don't get the money by tomorrow I'll kill Mwanga." And then he says to another caller: "Bring me the money tomorrow and I'll kill Mwanga right in front of you."'

'So tomorrow is Big Decision day,' said Nelson thoughtfully.

'At least we know Mwanga is still alive,'

said Benny.

'Any clues on where he is?' asked Nelson.

Mitch nodded. 'When Mwanga's name comes up the words "downstairs" and "basement" are used, so I think we can safely say that's where he is.'

'It would help to know where exactly in the basement,' put in Benny.

'I reckon he must be in a room near the main stairs,' said Mitch. 'At one point someone goes to take him some food, and there's not much time between him leaving and coming back.'

Nelson marked the four rooms on his plan that were nearest the bottom of the stairs. 'So, let's assume that he's in one of these,' he said.

Tug shook his head. 'I think you can cut out those two,' he said, pointing to the two larger rooms. 'They're too big. According to what Oba told us, one was a conference room, the other's a ballroom. Mwanga's a prisoner. They'll have put him in a small room, the nearest thing they've got to a cell.'

'Makes sense,' agreed Nelson. He put a cross by

the two smaller rooms. 'So, these are our targets. Right, let's sum up the whole situation as far as getting in.'

The six soldiers began to run through all the information they had gathered, but suddenly they heard the sound of vehicles.

Into view through the trees came a beaten-up open-topped 4x4, and immediately behind it came the jeep last seen at the village, with Adwana and two other villagers in the back. Their hands were tied and their faces bruised and cut from where they had been beaten.

Nelson turned angrily to Mitch. 'I thought you told them to get rid of the jeep,' he exclaimed.

'I did,' said Mitch. He groaned. 'They must have thought it was too good to dump.'

'And now they're paying the price,' muttered Benny.

The armed guards ran to meet the two vehicles, shouting and waving their rifles. The vehicles pulled up and the armed men in the jeep kicked and pushed Adwana and the other two men out on to the ground, shouting and jabbing their rifles threateningly at them the whole time.

'We have to save them,' whispered Two Moons.

Nelson shook his head. 'We can't,' he said. 'If we step in now we blow the operation. Our mission is to save Mwanga.'

A man came striding from the hotel. The unit realised from the way the armed men stepped back to clear a path for him that this must be the bandits' leader, Justis Ngola. Ngola was shorter than many of the men, but even from this distance he seemed to give off an energy and an impression of raw violence. Gold Headband – Ngola's cousin – was just a hoodlum by comparison.

Ngola was dressed in camouflage fatigues with army boots. On one hip was a handgun in a holster; on his other hip hung a machete.

The armed guards had stepped back to form a circle round Adwana and the two other bound men, who cowered on the ground. Ngola glared down at the men, and then shouted a question at them.

'What's he saying?' asked Nelson.

'He wants to know what happened to his cousin and the others.'

Adwana said something, obviously making an appeal, but Ngola cut it short by hitting Adwana across the face with the back of his hand and snapping something back at him.

'Adwana said he doesn't know,' Mitch translated. 'He says they found the jeep in the jungle and brought it back to their village. Ngola says he's lying.'

Ngola waved his fist threateningly at Adwana, and then fired off a burst of angry questions. Once again, Adwana appealed, but Ngola just kicked him in the ribs, making him double over in pain.

'Ngola wants to know where the Yankee soldiers are,' Mitch said. 'Adwana says he doesn't know any Yankee soldiers.'

Ngola snapped out an order, and his armed men hauled the three prisoners to their feet and dragged them to a group of trees. They tied each prisoner to one of the trees. Then Ngola pulled his handgun from his holster and stood in front of Adwana, shouting at him and pointing the gun directly at Adwana's face. Desperately, Adwana pulled at the ropes holding him to the tree trunk, shaking his head and begging. Even without Mitch translating it was obvious that Adwana was denying everything.

Ngola glared at him, and then suddenly turned towards the man tied to the tree next to Adwana, aimed his gun, and fired twice.

14

The sound of the two gunshots echoed through the jungle. The men of Delta Unit watched from their hiding place in angry silence as the villager Ngola had just killed slumped lifeless from the ropes that held him to the tree trunk. Blood dripped down from his body. Ngola's first shot had taken him in the chest, the second in the head.

Two Moons raised his rifle and aimed it at Ngola, but Nelson put his hand on the barrel and pushed it down, shaking his head.

'Not yet,' he whispered.

'Those people helped us!' snapped Two Moons.

'Our mission is to rescue Mwanga,' Nelson reminded him.

'We can shoot Ngola right now and rescue him!' insisted Two Moons.

'And take unnecessary casualties because the rest of his gang will know we're here?' countered Nelson. 'We can't fire-fight our way into a defended building like that. Not six against thirty. We've got to be clever about it.'

Two Moons scowled, then nodded. He knew Nelson was right, as did the rest of Delta Unit.

Ngola thrust the barrel of his gun into Adwana's face and shouted angrily at him again. Adwana looked terrified, but he shook his head, his voice desperate and pleading. Ngola smashed the gun into Adwana's face and blood poured from his nose and on to his torn shirt.

Then Ngola turned on his heel and stomped angrily back to the hotel. The unit didn't need Mitch's translation to understand that Ngola had been giving Adwana a warning: tell us what we want to know, or you and the other man will die as well. Two of the guards followed Ngola into the hotel.

The rest of his men stayed outside, laughing and jeering at Adwana and the other prisoner.

As they watched the bandits jeering, all of the men of Delta Unit had to fight the urge to burst out of their hiding place in the jungle and settle this issue once and for all. But freeing the two villagers wasn't their primary aim.

'Think they'll kill them?' asked Gaz.

'Not yet,' said Nelson. 'Alive, they're useful. Dead, they won't be able to give Ngola the information he wants.'

'From what I heard Ngola shouting at Adwana, he's going to let the night soften them up,' said Mitch. 'Spending the night in the dark, with the bad magic and the dead body of his friend next to him is bound to terrify Adwana. Ngola thinks that he will be ready to talk by morning and, if he doesn't, he'll kill one of them.'

'Looks like our timetable's being set for us,' said Nelson. 'Tomorrow, if Ngola gets his way, either the guys with the money turn up to buy Mwanga's freedom, or someone else turns up to have him killed. And also tomorrow morning Ngola plans to kill one of those two people who helped us, which we can't let happen.'

'So we go in tonight,' said Tug.

Nelson nodded. 'We go in tonight.'

15

'OK, I think we can say that this is going to be the situation: most of the bandits have drifted indoors, so it looks like five outside the building on guard, and all the rest inside, with Mwanga,' said Nelson. 'Rule one: let's make this as quiet an assault as we can. There are about twenty-five men inside that building. If we can do this without them realising what's going on, we should be able to get away without casualties. If we don't get Mwanga out of here alive, the whole operation has been a waste of time and men.'

The others nodded in agreement.

'Right,' said Nelson. 'Let's see what we need.'

'We need to cut the power to the hotel,' said Tug.

Everybody nodded in agreement. No power

meant no lights inside, so the men of Delta Unit, using night vision, would have an advantage.

'We take out the generator just before we go in,' said Nelson. 'Method?'

'A quiet explosive charge set off by remote control,' said Two Moons. 'That way we're in control of the timing.'

Benny jerked his thumb towards Adwana and the other villager tied to the trees.

'They've got to be released before we go in,' he said.

The others nodded in agreement.

'We'll need to take out the guards anyway, otherwise they'll present a problem when we come out,' said Mitch.

'Silent strike,' added Nelson. 'Silenced single-shot rifle, knife, wire, whatever.' He pointed to the sketch plan. 'OK, the guards are taken care of. Adwana and the other villager are released. The generator's knocked out. Two men stay outside the building as back-up – that'll be Benny and Two

Moons – while the four of us go in.'

Benny and Two Moons nodded.

'While you're outside you'll disable all the vehicles except two. I suggest you also plant plastic explosives on the other vehicles so that when we drive off you can blow them up. That way there'll be no noise while the actual operation's going on; just a load of big bangs as we leave.'

Two Moons grunted in agreement.

'We'll be using two vehicles for our getaway,' continued Nelson. 'We know the jeep the bandits used to bring Adwana here works and has fuel, and so does the other vehicle they turned up in. So I suggest those are the ones we take.

'Four of us go inside the building. Two men control the top of the stairs at ground level, making sure that the area is kept clear. That'll be Tug and Gaz. OK?'

Tug and Gaz nodded.

'Me and Mitch go down to the basement, find Mwanga and get him out. While all that's going on,

119

Benny and Two Moons start up the two vehicles so they're ready for us to jump on when we come out with Mwanga. Any questions?'

'Yes,' said Mitch. 'Although it's more of a concern than a question. The generator.'

'What about it?' asked Tug.

'Trust me, in this country those generators are always breaking down.'

'So?' asked Benny.

Nelson cursed. 'Damn!' he said. 'Good thinking, Mitch!'

Gaz frowned, puzzled. 'OK,' he said. 'Maybe I'm not the brightest penny in the box . . .'

'Torches!' explained Nelson with a groan. 'If the generator keeps breaking down, they'll have powerful torches ready.'

'And our night-vision goggles will be more of a hindrance than a help,' added Two Moons.

Bright light from a torch was the worst enemy of night-vision goggles. Even the smallest torch blinded anyone wearing night vision.

Two Moons turned to Mitch and grinned. 'Yeah! Good thinking, Mitch.'

'You'd all have made the connection,' said Mitch, shrugging.

'But only when someone started pumping bullets into us while we're blind,' Two Moons grunted.

'OK, so either we make sure the bandits don't suddenly start waving torches at us, or we go in without night vision, just ambient light,' said Nelson.

'We could lock them up,' suggested Gaz. He pointed to the receivers, which were still picking up sound and vision. 'It looks to me that quite a few of them are in the rooms we bugged.'

'And how do we lock them up?' asked Mitch.

Gaz grinned, produced his small pack of burglar tools and opened it. 'Lock-picks, pal. They can be used to lock a door as well as unlock it.'

Benny looked doubtful. 'It's risky,' he said. 'For one thing, we don't know if any of the doors still have locks on them, let alone whether they'll actually work.'

'It's worth a try,' said Nelson.

'If we can't lock the bandits in, we'll use flash bangs,' said Tug.

Flash bangs were stun grenades that produced intense white light and an incredibly loud noise when they exploded.

Nelson looked doubtful. Everyone knew what he was thinking. The noise would alert Ngola and the other guards, and once that happened it would be an open fire-fight inside the hotel.

'OK,' said Nelson. 'Flash bangs are a back-up. But only use them if you have to. That's it. Anything else?'

'Once we're away, where do we meet up?' asked Tug.

'Somewhere along the line,' said Nelson. 'Keep on the main road. We'll find each other.'

'And getting out of the country?' asked Benny. 'We've already said we can't trust anyone. Not even our own side.'

Nelson nodded thoughtfully. 'I'm working on

that,' he said.

'Will you have finished working on it by the time we go in?' asked Benny.

Nelson grinned. 'Maybe. Maybe not,' he said. 'But hopefully it'll be sorted by the time we need to get out of the country.'

16

Darkness fell.

Delta Unit lay ready in the long grass, equipped for a night assault: black Kevlar body-armour, full-face balaclavas beneath their protective helmets, night-vision goggles ready to be slipped over their faces, assault rifles with silencers and laser sights.

The three bandits guarding the front had given up any pretence of being a military fighting force and were sitting on the ground playing dice and drinking from bottles. The labels on the bottles looked as if they were half torn off.

'Some kind of local hooch,' whispered Mitch. 'If we're lucky, the guys inside will be drinking it as well. A few bottles of that and they won't be able to walk, let alone hold a gun.'

'Benny and Two Moons, you take out the guards at the back and prepare the generator as we planned,' said Nelson. 'Me, Tug and Gaz will take the guards at the front. Mitch, you'd better be the one who frees Adwana and tells him what's going on. We don't want him freaking out and giving the game away.'

Benny and Two Moons slipped into the darkness, heading for the back of the hotel.

Mitch slid along the ground towards the trees where Adwana and the other villager hung slumped from the ropes that tied them. Suddenly he stopped. The three bandits had stood up and were stumbling towards the prisoners, shouting and jeering.

Mitch now saw that Adwana and the other villager were still conscious. He could see the fear in their eyes as the bandits approached. These bandits were dangerous at the best of times. Drunk, they would be out of control, and Justis Ngola's order to keep the prisoners alive easily forgotten.

'We've got a problem,' Mitch whispered into his helmet microphone.

'We got it,' he heard Nelson's voice say confidently in his ear.

The three bandits were in front of Adwana now, lurching and jabbering insults. Then one of the bandits pulled a pistol from the holster at his hip and levelled it at the other villager. The villager strained at his ropes and twisted, fear and panic on his face.

The three bandits laughed.

Then Mitch heard three *phhtt!* sounds going off so close together they sounded like one shot.

The three bandits jerked like puppets on string; and then they crumpled to the ground.

Immediately Mitch ran from his cover to where Adwana and the other villager were tied, his knife already in his hand. He began cutting at the ropes. At the same time he whispered urgently for the two men to keep quiet.

'Say nothing!' he said.

He cut the ropes and Adwana and the other

man sank to the ground. Mitch reached down to help them, but they were already pushing themselves up.

'We're going to rescue Mwanga,' Mitch told them. 'You can wait and travel with us, or you can go now.'

'We go now,' Adwana murmered.

'But what about the magic in the jungle?' asked Mitch.

Adwana shuddered. 'Better the magic in the jungle than the devils in there!' he said, casting a fearful look at the building.

Nelson, Gaz and Tug joined Mitch. Adwana nodded at them, muttered something and then stumbled off into the jungle.

'What did he say?' asked Nelson.

'He thanked us,' said Mitch. 'And wished us good luck.'

Benny and Two Moons materialised near them.

'The guards at the back are out of action,' said Benny. 'The generator's ready to blow.'

'Good,' said Nelson. 'Wait till we're at the main entrance, then do it. As soon as we see the lights go out, we go in.'

17

Nelson, Mitch, Tug and Gaz stood in pairs at either side of the main entrance, assault rifles ready.

Mitch could see Benny crouched near one of the old vehicles. He guessed he was already fixing plastic explosive to it, most likely by one of the axles so that when it blew the wheel would come off and break the axle, making any immediate repair to get it going impossible.

Two Moons had slipped out of sight round the side of the hotel to set off the charges at the generator. From inside there were the sounds of men shouting, arguing, chattering, even some singing. It was a party of sorts. Maybe the bandits were already celebrating the money they expected to get as ransom for Mwanga.

Suddenly all the lights went out, both inside and outside the hotel. Immediately the four soldiers pulled their night-vision goggles down over their eyes and slipped inside.

The shouts and crashes that came from inside the rooms off the ground-floor hallway showed that the bandits had been caught by surprise by the sudden cut in power, no matter that it must have happened plenty of times before.

Gaz was already moving to the nearest door, his lock-picks in his hand. The door was partly open. Gaz pulled it shut quietly and then slid his lock-pick into the lock, turned it and heard a satisfying *click*.

Gaz looked over at Tug, who was standing watching, assault rifle poised, and gave him a thumbs-up. One door locked.

Swiftly Gaz moved on to the next door. This one was already shut but as Gaz got near to it, he saw the handle turn and the door begin to swing open inwards. Quickly Gaz grabbed the handle on his side and pulled it shut again. Then, holding the door firmly shut with one hand, he slid the lock-pick in and started to turn it. For one awful second the lock-pick stopped, jammed, and Gaz felt the door handle kicking against his hand as the person on the other side tried to pull the door open. Determined, Gaz held on with the iron grip of one hand while he tried again to turn the lock-pick with the other, all the time aware that if it didn't work soon he'd have to use a flash bang, putting the whole mission at risk.

Once again, the lock-pick jammed, and Gaz cursed silently. If he tried to force it, there was a good chance it would break, making it impossible to lock the other doors too.

Someone inside the room shouted angrily and Gaz felt the door being shaken violently. He gritted his teeth, tried to turn the lock-pick one last time, jiggling it slightly backwards and forwards, and this time he heard the cogs of the lock click into place.

Meanwhile Nelson and Mitch had made it down the stairs to the basement. They stood and listened in the darkness. There were no sounds from any of the rooms around them. Either they were empty, or their occupants fast asleep. In which case there should be no torches shining down here.

They glanced around them at the weird world of black and grey through the night-vision goggles.

Nelson indicated the two doors that opened on to the smallest rooms, according to the information Oba had given them. If their calculations were correct, they were pretty sure Mwanga would be in one of them. If they were wrong, then they had major problems.

Nelson checked the first door. It was unlocked, which suggested it was unlikely to be where Mwanga was held. He moved to the second door. This door had two heavy bolts on it, top and bottom. Cautiously he tested the handle. It wasn't locked. But it was bolted.

That made sense. If Ngola needed to get Mwanga out of here in a hurry, the last thing he'd want was to find that someone had lost the key to the room.

Nelson slipped both bolts back and pushed the door open, staying clear of the opening. A basic rule of survival. Never stand in an open doorway: all you do is make a perfect silhouetted target for any enemy waiting inside the room.

No gunfire sounded.

Nelson moved swiftly into the room, followed by Mitch, rifles ready.

A man was sitting in one corner, chained by his ankle to a radiator. Even with the grey fuzz of the night vision, they could see that it was Mwanga and that he had been badly beaten. His face was bruised and swollen. There were cuts above his eyes, and dried blood crusted down the sides of his face and around his mouth.

'Mr Mwanga?' said Nelson.

There was a muffled groan from the man.

'Mr Mwanga, we are here to rescue you,' said Nelson.

Swiftly he pulled out a pair of bolt cutters and severed the chain holding Mwanga to the radiator.

Mwanga struggled to get to his feet, but then fell back to the floor.

'I'll carry you,' said Nelson.

'No,' said Mwanga, his voice still thick with pain but sounding firm. 'I will walk.'

Once more he pushed himself up and stood unsteadily. He lurched forward, swaying, but obviously determined to get out on his own feet. He made it to the door, and then collapsed again, crashing to the floor.

'I'm sorry, Mr Mwanga, but we don't have time for this,' said Nelson.

He grabbed Mwanga and hauled him over one shoulder, then he headed back to the stairs, Mitch covering him all the way.

Just as they got there, the deafening sound of gunfire erupted from above them.

18

'Situation?' barked out Nelson as he and Mitch hurried up the stairs. Tug's voice came to them through their helmet headphones.

'They're shooting at the doors to open them. We're returning fire.'

More bursts of gunfire echoed through the building.

Nelson arrived at the top of the stairs first, Mwanga draped over his shoulders. Tug and Gaz fired at the now shattered doors to keep the bandits inside at bay, while Nelson ran for the main entrance.

A burst of returning fire came back through the splintered wood, and Gaz fell back, wincing with pain and clutching his left arm.

'Go with Nelson!' Mitch snapped. 'I'll take your position!'

Gaz was about to protest, but Mitch had already joined Tug and the two of them were firing round after round into the two rooms. Gaz nodded and ran after Nelson, gripping his left arm tightly to staunch the flow of blood.

There were now sounds above them, from the first floor, and Mitch moved to the bottom of the flight of stairs and fired off a couple of bursts, spraying them wide at the upper level. His bullets tore plaster from the walls and ripped through wooden partitions. Yells from above told Mitch he'd struck some targets. The main thing was to hold back any other bandits who were up there, to allow the unit time to get away.

'Let's go!' said Tug.

Tug joined Mitch at the foot of the stairs, and they headed for the main entrance. Both men moved side to side like crabs, Tug walking backwards to cover the rear, while Mitch edged forwards to cover the entrance.

More gunfire sounded from inside the hotel. No one appeared at first, then suddenly a door near them burst open and several men stumbled out. Through his night-vision goggles, Tug could see the guns in their hands. He pressed the trigger of his rifle, watching the bullets take out the first line of bandits. Finally they were outside and could see Nelson and Gaz in the back of the jeep with Mwanga. Benny was at the wheel, the engine racing.

Two Moons was standing up behind the wheel of the second vehicle, his rifle aimed at the hotel.

'OK! We're go!' snapped Nelson.

Immediately Benny let the clutch out and the jeep raced forward.

Mitch and Tug turned to face the hotel and kept up a stream of gunfire at the building to keep the bandits inside.

'Go!' yelled Tug.

Mitch ran towards the battered vehicle. Two Moons had already dropped down behind the steering wheel. A sudden yell of pain in Mitch's headphones made him jerk round. Tug was hit!

19

Some of the bandits were firing from an upstairs window and the ground around Tug seemed to jump as bullets thudded into it.

Mitch saw Tug crumple to the ground and immediately he rushed back, his rifle on automatic, rapid fire aimed at the upstairs window. Behind him he could hear the thunder of Two Moons' rifle as he stood on the jeep and poured tracer after tracer at the building as covering fire for Mitch.

Mitch reached Tug, who was struggling to sit up.

'Where are you hit?' he asked, kneeling down beside him.

'My left leg,' winced Tug. 'It's broken.'

'OK,' said Mitch. 'Grab my shoulders and grit your teeth. This is going to hurt.'

Mitch let his rifle swing from his shoulder by its strap, then he put both arms under Tug and hauled him up so that he was draped over his shoulder. Mitch stood up, lifting Tug as he did so. Tug groaned with the pain.

Mitch heard the engine of the vehicle coming closer, and realised that Two Moons was reversing towards him, holding the steering wheel with one hand, while still firing his rifle at the building with the other.

The jeep shuddered to a halt beside Mitch. He lowered Tug into the back of the vehicle as gently as he could, and then scrambled aboard himself before swinging his rifle level to fire again at the building.

'OK,' Mitch yelled. 'Let's take off!'

'As soon as I've let these babies go,' said Two Moons. 'Get your head down!' And he triggered the remote to set off the detonators of the explosives he'd rigged at the building and the other vehicles.

The effect was spectacular. All around them things exploded, pieces of metal hurtling in every direction. Roaring flames lit up the whole area, and Mitch could hear the yells of panic from the men inside the building.

'Bullseye!' yelled Two Moons triumphantly.

He dropped down behind the steering wheel, slammed the jeep into first gear and raced away, heading for the dirt road through the jungle. Mitch kept his attention on the hotel, now blazing, with smoke belching upwards, licking at the timber boards that covered the windows. Suddenly he saw a figure aiming something at the jeep. It looked like an RPG launcher.

Mitch swung his rifle at the figure and fired, but it was already too late. There was the dull thud and smoke of the RPG being fired, and then it hit the ground right next to the jeep's front offside wheel and exploded.

The jeep lurched violently with the force of the explosion, and then tilted and rolled. Mitch found himself flying through the air, still clinging to his rifle, then Tug's flying body crashed into him and the two men were flung to the ground. Mitch smacked his face against a rock, painfully jarring every part of his skull. He heard Tug yell out in pain and he struggled to lift himself up, but his mind was clouded, dazed. He was dimly aware of the sound of running feet getting nearer, and shouts and yells, and then something came down incredibly hard on the side of his head and everything went black.

20

Slowly Mitch came round. It was still night, though he could see by the light of the moon. His head throbbed. His face ached. It felt like it had been hit with lengths of hard wood.

He was tied to a tree, ropes binding his arms and legs, his wrists tied together.

He looked about him, even though every movement caused a searing pain in his neck. He wondered if he'd broken any bones. He knew that he was definitely hurt. Not just his face and neck – his whole body. His ribs. His arms. His legs.

'You're back with us?'

The voice was Two Moons'. Mitch strained his neck round and saw that Two Moons was also tied to a tree. They were the same trees that Adwana and the two villagers had been tied to. Two Moons had been stripped of his Kevlar body armour down to his combat trousers and boots. Mitch looked down at himself. He too was only wearing combat trousers and his boots.

'Yes,' said Mitch. His voice sounded muffled, far away. Maybe it was the after-effects of the RPG explosion. Sometimes temporary deafness followed.

'I guess you hurt all over,' said Two Moons.

Mitch started to nod, then stopped because of the pain in his neck. 'Yup,' he said.

'I thought you would. They gave you a pretty good kicking while you were unconscious. I was worried they might have kicked you to death.'

Mitch forced a rueful laugh. 'I guess they've got something extra special in mind for us,' he said. He looked at Two Moons, concerned. 'How about you?'

'Oh, they kicked me pretty good,' said Two Moons. 'Though not as bad as they did you. I guess

144

that's because I was still awake so I kept moving as much as I could.'

'Where's Tug?' asked Mitch.

Two Moons jerked his head towards an area that Mitch couldn't see. 'He's here,' he said. 'They got him tied to a tree too. But they let him sit down on the ground because of his broken leg.'

'Very thoughtful of them,' said Mitch drily.

'Not that thoughtful,' said Two Moons. 'They gave him a kicking too, and they beat him with their guns.'

'How is he?'

'Not good,' said Two Moons. 'He's unconscious, but alive. I can hear him groaning now and then, which is a good sign.'

Mitch's mind was clearing now and he was able to take in the situation better. They were tied facing the hotel. Black smoke still poured from the destroyed vehicles where the fuel lines had caught fire.

'You did a pretty good demolition job,' commented Mitch.

'I sure did,' grinned Two Moons. 'But I think it pissed off the opposition.'

Mitch took stock of the bandits who were hanging around. All of them looked angry. All of them were armed with rifles.

'Any sign of Ngola?' Mitch asked.

'He was here, watching them tie us up, and then he went off talking into his phone.'

Suddenly they could see movement: a group of bandits was hurrying towards them from the side of the hotel. As the group drew nearer, they parted, and the figure of Justis Ngola burst out from their midst and approached the Delta Unit soldiers. Immediately the rest of Ngola's bandits also came nearer, following their leader.

If Ngola had been furious before, when questioning Adwana and the two villagers, he was now enraged to the point of madness. His whole body seemed to be shaking as he stood there, his eyes jerking between Two Moons and Mitch. His mouth worked as if he couldn't get out the words of hatred that welled up inside him. Finally he seemed to gain control of himself, and he strode up to Mitch, thrust his angry face into the soldier's and demanded in English: 'Where have they taken Mwanga?'

Mitch looked coldly back at Ngola. 'My name is Paul Mitchell. My rank is Trooper. My number is –' he began.

His words were cut short as Ngola scowled and punched Mitch hard in the mouth. Mitch's head rocked back and smacked against the tree. Pain scorched through his head and he felt his mouth fill with blood.

'Where do you think you are, little man?' sneered Ngola. 'This is not your war. You are a criminal! A murderer! A thief! Do you know what we do to thieves?'

From his belt Ngola produced the vicious-looking machete. He waved the long blade in Mitch's face.

'We cut off the hands of thieves! We cut off the heads of murderers!'

Mitch forced himself to give a careless shrug. 'Better get on with it, then,' he said.

Ngola once more smashed his fist into Mitch's face. This time Mitch already had his head back against the tree to avoid his neck snapping back, but the force of the punch made his whole head throb and his ears ring.

Again Ngola thrust his face into Mitch's.

'Where have your people taken Mwanga?' he demanded for a second time.

'My name is Paul Mitchell. My rank is Trooper. My number is –'

And Ngola's fist connected with Mitch's face again, bringing tears of pain to Mitch's eyes. As his vision cleared, Mitch saw that Ngola was pointing the machete towards him, close to his throat.

'You think I will kill you and it will be a quick death for you,' said Ngola. 'Well, you are wrong. You will die slowly. I will chop off one finger at a time. And then your hands. And then your feet and legs. You think you will die from bleeding and it

148

will all be over.' Ngola shook his head. 'Every time I cut a piece off you I will put tar on it to stop the bleeding. You will not bleed to death. You will suffer. And eventually you will tell me. People always do. So why put yourself through all that pain? Tell me now. Where have your people taken Mwanga?'

'I don't know,' said Mitch. 'We weren't told. Only our commander knows that, in case any of us were taken prisoner.'

'Liar!' raged Ngola, and this time he stepped back from Mitch and swung the machete. The blade narrowly and deliberately missed.

'I can cut pieces off you with this so easily!' Ngola hissed. 'I am an expert. I have been using a machete since I was a small child. Want to see how good I am?'

'I'll take your word for it,' said Mitch.

Ngola hesitated, the machete swinging in his hand, his eyes boring into Mitch's, looking for the fear that he knew must be in there. Mitch looked back. He knew there was blood trickling down his chin from his nose and mouth, and every part of his body ached, but he was determined to stare right back at Ngola. Keep him wondering, gain some time.

He wondered where Nelson, Benny and Gaz were. Would they come back and try to rescue them? He didn't know. This was the first mission he'd been on with Delta Unit. In the SAS it was the practice to try to rescue your buddies if they were captured, but this was different. It was a different outfit, with a mission to rescue an important political figure and get him to safety. Mitch knew Nelson couldn't put Mwanga at risk, not when they'd achieved the first part of the mission. They were probably far away, working to get Mwanga safely out of the country.

Ngola stepped away from Mitch and glared at Two Moons, obviously weighing up his next move.

'One of you will tell me what I want to know,' he said. He pointed the machete at Two Moons, and then back at Mitch.

'I want you to think about what I am going to do to you with this machete. I want you to think about the pain you will suffer. I also want you to think about the pain you will be inflicting on the people of the village who helped you. Yes, I know they helped you! And when this is over I will go to the village and I will kill them all. Every last one. Every man, woman and child. There will be nothing left of them.

'Now, you can save yourself and everyone from all that pain by giving me just one simple answer. Where are your people taking Mwanga?'

'We don't know,' Mitch told him.

Ngola again shot angry looks at the Delta Unit soldiers and then said: 'I can see you don't believe me. Then I will show you how sincere I am about this.' He jerked the machete towards where Tug was lying. 'Your friend with the broken leg is no use to me. He is in too much pain to answer my questions sensibly. So I will use him as my example for you.'

Ngola rapped out an order in Igbo, and some of

151

his men disappeared from Mitch's line of vision. When they came back to where Mitch could see them they were dragging Tug's unconscious body. Tug's broken leg dragged behind him at a grotesque angle.

The men dumped Tug on the ground and then stepped back. Ngola stood over Tug and raised his machete.

'You will watch, and with every stroke you will see that I mean what I say.'

On the ground, Tug stirred, and then let out a moan of pain.

'You can still save your friend by telling me what I want to know,' said Ngola. 'This is your last chance.'

'We're telling you the truth,' said Two Moons. 'We don't know where they've taken him. That wasn't our remit.'

'In that case,' growled Ngola angrily, 'see what I do to people who defy me!' And he raised the machete.

21

The sound of a phone suddenly rang out.

This can't be happening, thought Mitch. This is some kind of dream. We're in the jungle! We're about to be killed. And now a phone rings!

Mitch realised it was Ngola's satellite phone. Ngola snatched it up eagerly and listened to what the caller said, then replied urgently in Igbo. The caller said something that brought a smile to Ngola's face. He barked a reply into the phone, but his manner was more relaxed now. He listened a bit longer, still smiling, and then he finished the call. He turned to Mitch and Two Moons.

'Well!' he announced, not even trying to conceal his delight. 'It seems my people have found the jeep your friends used to get away. Which means it won't be long before we have them and Mwanga back here.

'But the real bonus is that I have found a buyer for the three of you. Hard cash from someone who wants you.'

'Why?' asked Mitch.

'You will be able to ask them that question yourself shortly,' said Ngola. 'But, as I understand it, they want you so that they can kill you themselves, in front of some film cameras. Your deaths will be shown on televisions around the whole world.'

Ngola smiled.

'This has turned out well for me! Soon my people will find Mwanga and bring him back to me. And I earn even more money from capturing you!'

He barked something at his men, and then walked away towards the hotel.

Two Moons was aware that Mitch had suddenly become more alert than before.

'What's up?' he asked.

'Ngola's just told his men they can cut off our

hands, but to leave us alive afterwards. They'll only need our faces on camera. It's his sick idea of getting revenge against us for what we did here.'

Ngola's men had gathered in a small huddle, and were chattering away rapidly. Three of them had already taken machetes from their belts.

'What's going on now?' asked Two Moons.

'They're arguing over who gets first chop,' said Mitch. He listened to a bit more of the argument, and then let out a heavy sigh as the bandits knelt down in a small circle.

'What?' asked Two Moons.

'They're going to play dice for the pleasure,' Mitch told him. 'The winner gets to choose which one of us he wants to cut a hand from.'

'Think I can get a bet on?' joked Two Moons. 'I'm usually good at picking a winning hand.'

Despite himself, the pain he was in, and their dreadful situation, Mitch couldn't help but laugh at this.

'You are one crazy Sioux,' he said.

As they watched the crouching men throw dice, Two Moons asked: 'You think Ngola was telling the truth? About his people finding the jeep?'

'I don't know,' replied Mitch. 'Why would he make it up?'

'To make us think they were closing in.'

Mitch frowned. 'But say they have found the jeep. Why would Nelson abandon it? They've got Mwanga with them. They need transport.'

'Maybe they found another set of wheels,' suggested Two Moons.

'Maybe,' agreed Mitch. Then he tensed as raised and excited voices came from the dice players. 'This is it,' he said.

'What is?'

'One of them's just won.'

The bandits stood up from their huddle, and one of them took a machete and walked towards the bound Delta Unit soldiers, a big smile on his face. The other bandits followed him, chattering delightedly.

'Do you know who he chose?' asked Two Moons.

Mitch gave a sigh. 'Yes,' he said. 'The English one.'

'So that's you or Tug.'

'They haven't heard Tug speak yet, so they don't know he's English,' said Mitch. 'I think he's chosen me.'

As if by way of confirmation, two of the other bandits suddenly fell on Mitch and held him, while a third hacked away at the ropes that tied his wrists together. As soon as Mitch's wrists were free, one of the bandits grabbed his left arm and pushed it out to the side, gripping it firmly with both hands. Mitch tried to pull his hand back, twisting his arm as hard as he could, but it was no use – the bandit had Mitch's arm in a tight grip. The lucky winner let out a delighted yell and swung the machete blade back.

22

Mitch never heard the shot. It must have come from a silenced weapon. All he knew was that one moment the machete was in the air, about to cut his hand off, and then the bandit was spun round by the force of a bullet tearing into him.

Then there was more firing, all of it silenced, and the bandits nearest to them fell, shot with deadly accuracy.

The other bandits began scrambling for their rifles, but they too were cut down.

A voice just behind Mitch said, 'We didn't mean to cut it that close.'

Nelson!

Then Gaz's Geordie accent joined in with: 'Still, better late than never, that's what I always say.'

Nelson was already cutting through the ropes that bound Mitch and Two Moons, while Gaz stood in a half-crouch, alert for every movement, his rifle ready against any further attack.

Mitch pointed at the unconscious Tug, lying on the ground. 'Be careful with him. His leg's broken and he's been badly beaten.'

'Where's Mwanga?' asked Two Moons.

'Safe,' said Nelson. 'Benny's minding him.'

'I thought you'd been shot,' Mitch commented to Gaz.

'I'm always getting shot,' Gaz chuckled. 'Nothing a bit of first aid couldn't deal with.'

Suddenly Mitch was aware of a noise overhead, approaching fast. It was a helicopter.

'This might be a problem,' he said. 'Ngola's sold us. These could be his buyers.'

Gaz chuckled. 'No, pal. This is our taxi.'

'What?'

'I'll explain later,' said Nelson. 'Let's just get on board and get out of here.'

The helicopter was now right overhead and descending, its lights and the whirr of its rotor blades filling the area. The men watched as it touched down.

'Not yet,' said Mitch grimly. 'Ngola's still alive.'

Mitch moved forward and picked up one of the rifles near the dead body of one of the bandits, but Nelson stepped firmly in his path.

'We don't have time for this,' snapped Nelson. 'Our job is to get Mwanga to safety. We can leave Ngola for another time.'

'There won't be another time,' said Mitch. 'If he gets away, Ngola will tear Adwana's village apart and kill everyone in it for revenge.'

'Saving the village is not part of our mission,' said Nelson.

'Well, it's part of mine,' said Mitch, checking the ammunition rounds in the rifle.

Nelson glared at him. 'If you go you'll be dis-obeying an order from your commanding officer,' he snapped.

'I'm sorry,' said Mitch shortly. 'I've got to do this.'

With that he stepped round Nelson and hurried towards the hotel.

23

Nelson glared after the retreating figure of Mitch. 'I'll have him court-martialled for this!' he snarled.

'Absolutely right, Colonel,' grinned Two Moons. 'And for that you need him alive. So I guess I'd better go after him.'

Two Moons bent down and scooped up his rifle.

Nelson grabbed him by the arm. 'I can give you ten minutes max, Two Moons,' he said firmly. 'After that, you'd better be back here, with or without Mitch, because that chopper's taking off. One second after ten minutes, we're gone! Getting Mwanga to safety is our first priority. I can't risk a fire-fight with Ngola's reinforcements.'

'I hear you, Colonel,' replied Two Moons.

He hurried towards the hotel after Mitch.

*

Mitch came running back out of the hotel as Two Moons arrived at the main entrance.

'Ngola and the rest of his men have gone,' he said. 'The helicopter must have freaked them.'

'So he's out in the jungle somewhere?' asked Two Moons. 'Think his men are with him?'

'I don't know,' said Mitch. 'But I doubt they're in a big group – too easy to spot. Anyway, Ngola is the dangerous one. He's the one I'm after.'

Two Moons looked at his watch. 'The colonel said we can have ten minutes, then the chopper leaves. We've got eight minutes left.'

'Then why are we wasting time talking?' demanded Mitch. He pointed towards a track. 'I'll take that way.' He pointed towards another, further on. 'You take that one.'

Two Moons nodded and they hurried off towards the dark jungle.

At the jungle's edge Mitch stood in the darkness and listened. He wondered how far in Ngola had gone; he may have been the sort who scoffed at tales of bad magic but he would know how deadly the jungle was at night. The predators. The swamps. If Mitch guessed right, Ngola would be hiding in the fringes of the jungle, still near to the hotel area.

Without his usual protective Special Forces gear, Mitch knew he was vulnerable. No radio. No protective helmet or night vision. No Kevlar body armour. No weapons other than a rifle he'd taken from a dead bandit.

This was how it had been for warriors of days gone by, the stories Mitch had grown up on as a boy: one against one in the darkness of the jungle. Mitch kept moving, eyes and ears alert for any sound. Suddenly he heard footsteps just behind him, and he whirled round, rifle raised, his finger poised on the trigger.

Two Moons pushed the barrel of Mitch's rifle to one side. 'Ngola ain't that way,' he said. He looked at his watch. 'We got five minutes left.'

'I'll see you at the chopper,' said Mitch. 'If I'm not there, go without me.'

With that, he moved further into the jungle. By now his eyes had grown accustomed to the ambient light coming from the helicopter and the dying fires from the explosions.

Ngola was here somewhere. Lying in wait. Mitch could feel him.

He squatted down and listened, trying to identify the different sounds he could hear: nocturnal animals; birds moving in the trees, roosting for the night; the sounds of swamps and insects. Add to that the constant background hum from the chopper. The jungle was alive with noise.

Mitch felt a sense of anger and frustration. He knew his chances of finding Ngola were very slim. If Ngola was here and watching him, all the bandit had to do was keep one step ahead, or just lie low and wait for Mitch to blunder into his position.

Nelson was right. This was a wild-goose chase. This was Ngola's home territory; he could hide here for a long time. And the longer Mitch waited, the more the clock ticked towards the chopper leaving. If he wanted to get home alive, he should be on the chopper. But Mitch couldn't shake his feeling of responsibility to Adwana and the other villagers. If he left the jungle now, Ngola and his men would carry out their threat and all the villagers would die, butchered horribly.

He wondered how long he had left. He was sure Nelson's original ten minutes must be up. And then he heard the sound of the chopper's engine change as it engaged. He could feel the downdraught of the rotors through the trees and the lights rising in the night sky. The helicopter was leaving.

He hoped Two Moons had made it back in time. Mitch was sure he had: Two Moons had been with Nelson for two years, so he'd know that when Nelson said something, he meant it. And, as Nelson had said right from the start, the aim of the mission was to rescue Mwanga and get him to safety. Delta Unit had gone; Mitch was on his own.

24

Mitch strained his ears for sounds that would give Ngola away. He listened for boots cracking on twigs. For guns being cocked.

Ngola had a machete and a pistol. He seemed to favour the machete, but he would have to be close to his enemy to use it. A pistol killed from a distance. But that meant getting a clear shot. Here in the jungle, at night, that wouldn't be so easy.

Mitch hefted the rifle in his hands. It was an FN FAL with a twenty-round magazine. He'd used one before; it was a good weapon. The magazine felt half empty, so he guessed he had about ten bullets. He made sure the rifle was on single shot.

Suddenly he heard a noise. A rustle in the trees, then footsteps approaching. More than one.

He crouched down, his finger on the trigger, ready to fire as soon as he saw Ngola. Then, through the ambient light still coming from the fires and burning wreckage, Mitch saw Ngola with a group of his armed bandits pushing their way through the undergrowth, heading back towards the hotel. They must have felt it was safe to return now the helicopter had gone.

Mitch raised the rifle and took sight. He cursed. He couldn't get a clear shot as Ngola was surrounded by about six men. He'd have to get rid of the ones in the way first before he could take out Ngola.

He fired twice, and hit his targets both times. Two men crumpled to the ground, yelling in pain as his bullets struck home. Ngola stopped and swung round, and in the half-light Mitch could see the expression of shock on his face as he looked down at the two fallen men.

Got you! thought Mitch triumphantly as he held Ngola firmly in his sights and pulled the trigger.

The gun jammed.

'Damn!' cursed Mitch.

He pulled the trigger again, but the bullets were stuck. Either the bandit whose gun it had been hadn't looked after it, or he'd stuffed the wrong size ammo in the magazine. Mitch heard shouting and realised that Ngola had recovered and was screaming orders at his men, ordering them to scatter and search the jungle.

Then Ngola's voice yelled out: 'Hear me, Yankee!'

He's got that wrong, thought Mitch.

'The fact you didn't shoot me after you killed my men means your gun is useless!' continued Ngola.

But he's got that one right, mused Mitch.

'If you give yourself up, I will give you a quick and easy death!' Ngola shouted. 'But if you make me come and find you, your death will be more painful than you can imagine!'

There was silence, and then Ngola shouted: 'Very well! You wish to die painfully!'

With that, he shouted more orders, and his

men began to crash through the jungle in search of Mitch.

Great! thought Mitch sourly. He looked at the FAL rifle in his hands, and cursed silently again. A good weapon, ruined by some idiot! Now it was only useful as a club.

The sounds of Ngola's men's boots were getting nearer. If he started to run, they'd hear him crashing through the undergrowth and they'd start shooting. Even firing blind, with automatic fire there was a good chance that some of their bullets would hit him.

Mitch scanned the area immediately around him, and saw a dark patch of water. A jungle swamp. He didn't know how deep it was, or what dangers might be lurking in the stagnant water, but it was the only protection he had on offer right now.

He slid on his belly to the edge of the swamp and let himself sink into the stinking, thick muddy water. He took the FAL in with him. The firing mechanism was already jammed, so mud inside it wouldn't make it any more useless than it already was.

He sank further. The water was deeper than he'd thought, and now it came right up to his neck. He reached out and grabbed hold of a nearby tree root, just as his head sank beneath the surface. No sooner had he submerged than he felt the thudding vibration of boots crashing past, shaking the tree root and rippling the thick oozing water. He stayed beneath the water, holding his breath, mouth closed firmly.

He could feel water insects and leeches on his skin, eager for fresh food. They crept over his body, along his arms, digging into the skin of his neck and back.

Mitch stayed under as long as he could. He'd have to take a chance and put his head out to get some air soon. He couldn't feel any more vibrations, but that didn't mean that Ngola's men weren't near by, maybe even watching this jungle pond.

Carefully, slowly, Mitch eased his head out of the

water, taking in a breath gratefully as his nose and mouth broke the surface.

There was no one around. Ngola's men had gone.

Mitch stayed with the rest of his body beneath the water and listened for a while longer, letting his eyes get used to the jungle half-light again.

He could make out some of Ngola's men back in the grounds of the hotel. The rest were probably still searching for him in the jungle.

The hotel itself was still in semi-darkness, so he guessed they hadn't been able to repair the generator yet.

Where was Ngola? Again, Mitch guessed that he'd be back inside the hotel, talking on his satellite phone, trying to salvage the situation. No doubt he was pretending to his customers that he still had Mwanga and the soldiers as his prisoners.

Mitch pulled himself clear of the water and slid on to the earth. He was covered from head to foot in black slime, and was armed only with a rifle that didn't work. But he had promised himself that he would protect the villagers who'd helped them, so he was going to find Ngola even if it was the last thing he did.

25

Mitch weighed up his situation. The rifle he had didn't work, but there would be better weapons inside the hotel. If he dumped the rifle on the ground here and Ngola's men found it, they would be able to track his movements and discover he was heading for the hotel. He wanted Ngola to think he was on the run in the jungle, so he slid the rifle into the jungle pond and let it sink out of sight beneath the murky water. There would be no trace of it. But now he was completely unarmed. If caught, he couldn't even bluff his way out of trouble.

Mitch crouched down just inside the edge of the jungle and studied the hotel. In the dim light he could see that some of the windows had been uncovered during the fire-fight, the wooden boards and sheets of iron dangling and broken. One of those windows would be the best way in. He settled on one with no light at all coming from it. No light meant no torches, which he hoped meant no one was inside.

Some of Ngola's men were still out in front of the hotel. He could see a couple at the back, by what remained of the generator, shining torches on it and examining it for damage.

Good, he thought. That will keep them occupied. So long as they don't turn those torches my way.

He crept low and fast from the jungle to the unguarded side hotel wall. He dropped down in the grass beneath the dark broken window and strained his ears for any sound from within. There was nothing.

Mitch stood up carefully, keeping alert the whole time for any movements. He checked the window. In one corner of it, the glass had been smashed out. Mitch carefully pushed the dangling wooden board to one side, pulled himself up to the window sill, and then slid into the room.

Once inside, he knelt on the floor, his vision adjusting to the dim light. He heard sounds from outside, and from the rooms nearby. Then he heard Ngola's voice, loud and commanding. It came from somewhere upstairs. Wherever he was, the door of the room was open because his voice was perfectly audible. Then Ngola stopped shouting and Mitch heard a door slamming and boots crashing down the stairs.

He hurried over to the door and peered through the crack. One of Ngola's men was coming. The man went into the room opposite where Mitch was. Immediately a hubbub of voices broke out, but was muffled as the door shut.

The men were worried about their money. That much Mitch had heard before the door closed. With Mwanga gone, there would be no ransom.

Mitch guessed Ngola was already planning his next scheme. Another kidnapping probably. Maybe foreign workers on the oil fields. The oil firms usually paid up, if the worker taken was vital to them.

This came to an end for Ngola now, vowed Mitch. But he needed a weapon.

He scanned the room. It was a shambles. There were pieces of broken furniture and wrecked chairs everywhere, and a collapsed wooden table with only three legs remaining. Mitch went to the table and picked up the fourth leg from where it lay on the floor. It felt heavy. It would make a good club.

Then his eyes caught a glint in the half-light: something metal on the floor near one of the walls. Mitch moved over to it. It was a knife.

He picked it up and felt it in his hand. It was double-bladed with a sharp point and a good hilt. Well balanced if it needed to be thrown. At a distance it was no match for a gun, but up close it would be silent and deadly. But first he had to get near to Ngola. And alone, without any of Ngola's men around to defend him.

He was about to put the table leg back down on

the floor when he stopped. A weapon was a weapon. A club and a knife. They could both be useful.

Mitch peered out through the crack in the door again, checking the hallway and the stairs. No one was there. Silently he opened the door wider and slid out, then padded across to the stairs and began to climb them. He had thought of taking off his boots to make himself as silent as possible. Then he considered the other possibilities: treading on broken glass from the fire-fight, having his feet slashed at with a machete. He decided to keep his boots on.

He made it to the top of the stairs. The first-floor landing went in both directions, left and right. Which way would lead him to Ngola? And which room? If he blundered into the wrong one and came face to face with a bunch of Ngola's armed bandits, he was as good as dead.

26

Suddenly a phone rang out. Ngola's satellite phone again! Coming from one of the rooms to the left.

Mitch moved noiselessly along the corridor until he came to a door from behind which he heard Ngola's voice, bargaining, still offering the death of Mwanga 'at a good price'. Mitch pushed the knife into the belt of his trousers. He held the broken table leg firmly in his right hand and his left went to the door handle. Slowly, he turned the handle and pushed it gently, just a crack, enough to hear Ngola's voice clearer and to know that the door hadn't been locked.

Ngola was still talking on his phone. Good, thought Mitch. His attention will be on the conversation.

Mitch pushed open the door and stepped in, swinging his gaze around the room to see if anyone else was there. Ngola was alone.

Ngola turned, and as he saw Mitch his mouth dropped open.

I must look like some nightmare creature from the swamp, thought Mitch grimly, covered from head to toe in slimy mud.

Ngola recovered and his hand reached for the pistol that lay on the top of a large desk near him. Mitch acted quickly, hurling the broken table leg straight at Ngola. It struck the bandit leader full in the face and he fell backwards with a yell. Mitch leapt forward, reaching for the pistol, but Ngola reacted, throwing the table leg at the gun. The gun went skidding off the desk, sliding into a jumble of papers and clothes and then disappearing between some shelves and the wall.

Mitch turned towards the shelves, but Ngola was shouting for help from his men. Swiftly, Mitch kicked the door shut, then yanked another heavy wooden desk across the door. That would hold them back for a short while. So long as it was enough time to finish Ngola.

Ngola had scrambled back to his feet and thrown himself towards the shelves, tearing at them, searching for the fallen gun. Mitch took the knife from his waistband and lunged at Ngola. Ngola saw the movement and twisted himself back, the blade narrowly missing him.

He ran for the door. For a moment Mitch thought he was going to pull the desk away, but instead Ngola had snatched something up from near it. Now he stood and smiled triumphantly at Mitch. In his hand was his machete.

'You have a knife,' he sneered, 'but it is nothing against a machete!'

Ngola's men had arrived outside now and were shouting and pushing against the door, trying to force the desk away from it.

Ngola moved towards Mitch, swinging the machete, a smirk on his face.

I'm in trouble, thought Mitch. This guy's an expert with that, and he's dead right that a knife is no match for a machete in a hand-to-hand fight. If he gets close . . .

Ngola gave a yell, triumph mixed with rage, and swung the machete back ready to strike as he lunged powerfully at Mitch. Mitch took his chance and threw the knife hard. The point hit Ngola full on in the throat.

Ngola stopped, dropped the machete and stumbled, his eyes staring at Mitch in amazement, his mouth opening and closing, unable to speak. Mitch bent down and scooped up the fallen machete, and with one swift slash delivered the fatal blow. Ngola toppled to the floor.

From outside the door the shouting and banging increased. Then came the sound of loud machine-gun fire. Mitch looked towards the window, the only way out. But that window was barred by a protective iron sheet fixed firmly across it. There was no way he would get through it before the bandits shot their way in.

Then he realised with a shock that the shooting and shouting had stopped.

'OK, Mitch, you can open this door now!' called a familiar voice.

It was Two Moons!

27

Mitch hauled the heavy desk away from the door, and opened it to reveal Two Moons, Gaz and Nelson, all carrying automatic rifles. The bodies of dead bandits littered the corridor.

Mitch stared at them, stunned. Gaz and Two Moons were grinning at his look of astonishment, but Mitch could tell from the very grim expression on Nelson's face that the colonel was furious with him.

Two Moons looked down at the dead body of Ngola.

'Wow. You really got him,' he said.

'Let's do the compliments later,' said Nelson tersely. 'The chopper should be coming back soon. This time we're going to be on it.'

As Mitch followed the others along the landing and down the stairs, he could see more bandits' bodies. The guys had done a massive clear-up job.

'The chopper took Mwanga and Tug for treatment,' explained Gaz. 'Benny went with them to make sure everything's OK. We stayed to look for you. Once we heard all hell breaking loose inside the hotel, we knew that's where you must be.'

'But Nelson said –' began Mitch.

'The colonel says lots of things,' said Two Moons. 'But one thing is always true: we don't leave our men behind.'

By now they had come out of the hotel and Mitch could hear the familiar whirring of a helicopter's rotors, its lights fast approaching.

Whatever consequences Mitch might face, they'd rescued Mwanga, Ngola was dead, and the villagers were safe. The mission was over.

The helicopter took them over the jungle, past the lights of the oilfields around the Niger Delta and across the open sea to where a US warship was waiting for them.

Nelson sat at the front with Two Moons. Mitch sat with Gaz. He was uncomfortably aware that Nelson hadn't exchanged a word with him since they left the room and Ngola's dead body.

'I guess I'm in the colonel's bad books,' he said.

'You disobeyed a direct order, Mitch,' said Gaz. 'You know what the military are like about orders.'

'Yeah,' admitted Mitch. He looked again at Nelson, at the angry expression on the colonel's face. Then he frowned, puzzled.

'This chopper . . .' he said.

'What about it?' asked Gaz.

'The colonel said he didn't trust anybody. So where did it come from?'

'The colonel said he didn't trust anyone *on our side*,' emphasised Gaz. He jerked his thumb at the pilot. 'This is sort of a private arrangement between the colonel and some old ex-army buddy of his. Turns out the guy's working as a pilot for one of the oil companies.'

'But how did the colonel get hold of him?'

Gaz shrugged. 'I don't ask those sort of questions,' he said. 'Just be grateful he did.'

The chopper landed on the flight deck of the warship. Benny was waiting for them. 'Glad you made it,' he said. He gave Mitch a broad grin. 'Man, you sure are dirty!'

'How are Mwanga and Tug?' demanded Nelson.

'They're in sick bay. Both doing fine,' Benny said.

'Good,' said Nelson. He turned to Mitch, his face still unsmiling. 'Go get cleaned up. Then I want to see you, Mitch. I'll be in the captain's cabin. Report to me there in an hour.'

With that, Nelson headed for the hatch that led below decks.

Gaz sighed ruefully. 'Somehow, from his tone, I don't think you're in line for a medal, pal,' he said.

An hour later, showered and changed, Mitch knocked at the door of the captain's cabin.

'Come in!' called Nelson.

Mitch entered.

The cabin, like most on the warship, was small and the large figure of Nelson seemed to fill it. He was sitting at a small table.

'You know what this is about, don't you,' said Nelson. It wasn't a question; it was a statement. His tone, like the expression on his face, was grim and hard.

'Me going after Ngola,' said Mitch.

Nelson nodded. 'You put the operation at risk. We had Mwanga on board the chopper. We'd come back to pick up the rest of the unit. We were all ready to get everyone to safety, and you rush off on some private vendetta.'

'While Ngola stayed alive, those villagers were in danger.'

'In a battle zone everyone's in danger, whatever happens,' snapped back Nelson. 'The point is that you disobeyed a direct order from your commanding officer. In army terms, that's mutiny. I should have shot you dead as soon as you headed for the jungle. I'd have been within my rights, and you know it.'

Mitch hesitated, then he nodded. 'Yes, sir,' he said.

'I don't need your agreement!' barked Nelson angrily. 'It's a fact! You didn't just put the mission in jeopardy, but also the lives of your fellow soldiers.' He shook his head sadly. 'You're a maverick, Mitch. You're a fine warrior, but a bad soldier. I don't want you on my team.'

As he heard these words, Mitch felt his heart sink.

After being out of the game he had been reluctantly drawn back in. And he'd found a comradeship with Two Moons and Gaz that really meant something to him. As part of Delta Unit, he'd felt at home for the first time in a long while. The Band of Brothers. And now it was being snatched away from him.

'But Tug does,' added Nelson.

Mitch looked at Nelson, shocked. 'Tug?' he echoed.

Nelson nodded. 'And Benny. And Two Moons and Gaz. They seem to think I ought to overlook this and give you another chance.'

'Tug and Benny?' repeated Mitch, still stunned by what he had heard. He could understand Two Moons and Gaz speaking up for him, but Tug and Benny? It didn't make sense.

'So, although, as you know, this outfit is not a democracy and orders are orders, that gives you four votes of confidence against one. So, what do you say? Can I trust you?'

'Yes, sir,' said Mitch.

'You'll obey orders?'

'Yes, sir,' repeated Mitch, more firmly this time.

'OK,' said Nelson. 'In that case, consider yourself part of the team. But this is a test period. I'll be watching you, Mitch. You screw up like that again, you're out. Is that clear?'

'Yes, Colonel.'

Tug was lying in a bed, a cage over his legs, as Mitch entered the medical quarters. Drips and tubes were running into him.

'How's the leg?' asked Mitch.

'It'll be worse when the anaesthetic wears off and the pain kicks in,' said Tug. 'I'm glad you came by. I didn't get the chance to thank you for coming back for me.'

'I'm the one to say thanks,' said Mitch. 'Colonel Nelson was going to kick me out of the unit. He says you spoke up for me.'

Tug shrugged. 'It seemed the right thing to do,' he said.

'Because I came back for you?'

Tug nodded. 'It showed me you'd put yourself in danger for a comrade. It means we can count on you if things go wrong.'

'That's what soldiers do,' Mitch said.

Tug forced a smile.

'That's what soldiers are *supposed* to do. But

when it comes to it, not all do.' He held out his hand to Mitch. 'You came through for us.'

Mitch took Tug's hand and shook it. 'Thanks,' he said.

'Welcome to Delta Unit,' said Tug.

CONFIDENTIAL
X 53561
ENCLOSURES

DISPATCHED
N.S.C.

Jun 29 3 02 PM '61

I. G.

978-1-4052-4780-1

CONFIDENTIAL
(Classification)

NAME: Paul Mitchell

KNOWN AS: Mitch

USUKCSF UNIT: Delta

RANK: Trooper

PLACE OF BIRTH: London, England, UK

HEIGHT: 5' 11"

LANGUAGES: English, French, Dutch, various West African languages (Yoruba, Ibo etc.)

PREFFERED WEAPON: Heckler & Koch Mark 23 pistol

SPECIALISM: extreme terrain

CONFIDENTIAL
(Classification)

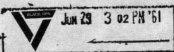

DISPATCHED
N. S. C.

JUN 29   3 02 PM '61

I. G.

978-1-4052-4780-1

CONFIDENTIAL

NAME: Charles Nelson

KNOWN AS: Colonel

USUKCSF UNIT: Delta

RANK: Colonel

PLACE OF BIRTH: Boston, Massachussetts, USA

HEIGHT: 6' 0"

LANGUAGES: English, Chinese, Russian, Korean

PREFFERED WEAPON: Smith & Wesson .38 Bodyguard pistol

SPECIALISM: leadership, diplomacy

978-1-4052-4780-1

NAME: Tony Two Moons

KNOWN AS: Two Moons

USUKCSF UNIT: Delta

RANK: Sergeant

PLACE OF BIRTH: Arizona, USA

HEIGHT: 5' 11"

LANGUAGES: English, Inuit, Spanish, Japanese

PREFFERED WEAPON: Ingram Model 10 sub-machine gun

SPECIALISM: ordnance, explosives

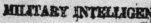
MILITARY INTELLIGEN

I. G.

and; include

NAME: Robert Tait

KNOWN AS: Tug

USUKCSF UNIT: Delta

RANK: Captain

PLACE OF BIRTH: Oxford, England, UK

HEIGHT: 5' 7"

LANGUAGES: English, Pushtu, Farsi, Hindi, Turkish

PREFFERED WEAPON: Walther P99 pistol

SPECIALISM: leadership, diplomacy

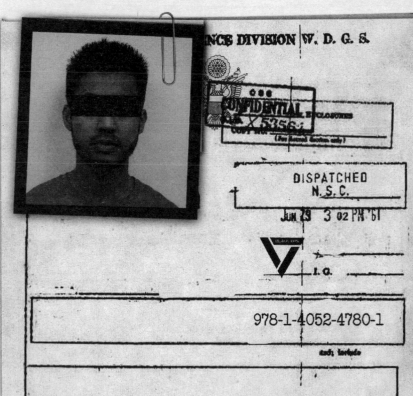

INTELLIGENCE DIVISION W. D. G. S.

CONFIDENTIAL

DISPATCHED
N.S.C.

JUN 29 3 02 PM '61

I. O.

978-1-4052-4780-1

CONFIDENTIAL

NAME: Bernardo Jaurez

KNOWN AS: Benny

USUKCSF UNIT: Delta

RANK: Lieutenant

PLACE OF BIRTH: Houston, Texas, USA.

HEIGHT: 5' 7"

LANGUAGES: English, Spanish, Polish, Greek

PREFFERED WEAPON: Ruger 0.38 Service-Six pistol.

SPECIALISM: tactics

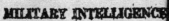

CONFIDENTIAL
(Classification)

DISPATCHED
N.S.C.

Jun 29   3 02 PM '61

978-1-4052-4780-1

I. G.

CONFIDENTIAL
S.I.B. X 53561
(For Local Section only)

NAME: Danny Graham

KNOWN AS: Gaz

USUKCSF UNIT: Delta

RANK: Trooper

PLACE OF BIRTH: Newcastle, England, UK

HEIGHT: 5' 6"

LANGUAGES: English, German, Italian, Norwegian

PREFFERED WEAPON: Beretta 93R pistol

SPECIALISM: recon, stealth, surveillance